JUUHHHUUUU

MANOJ KUMAR SHARMA

INDIA • SINGAPORE • MALAYSIA

ISBN 979-8-88815-613-1

Disclaimer

Reader friends and others, please note that this is a work of fiction. The characters, places, businesses, technologies, practices, events, incidents, and everything else mentioned in the book are the products of the author's imagination and have been used in a fictitious manner. Any resemblance to any person, living or dead, place, location, business, incident, event, practice or technology is purely coincidental and the author cannot be held responsible for the same. Reader friends and others are requested to treat the essence of this story as fictional material and nothing more than that.

DEDICATION

This Anthology Book is dedicated to my mother, Late Hem Lata.

This Anthology Book is also dedicated to True-Lovers in the whole world.

CONTENTS

Acknowledgement 9

Preface 11

Prologue 13

Chapter 1: Accidented Souls 27

Chapter 2: Immersions, Emersions, Emotions 69

Chapter 3: Virtual Valentina 113

ACKNOWLEDGEMENT

Thanks, from the bottom of my heart:

- To my nation "India"
- To all the book lovers
- To my family
- To my friends

PREFACE

At first glance, the peculiarity of the title 'JUUHHHUUUU' intrigues the reader. But, once they start sailing into the fictional world of the book, that tickling mystery unveils.

'JUUHHHUUUU' brings three short stories in peculiar self-styled storytelling by someone unavoidably lovable. Each story takes the reader on a voyage in the rarest life circumstances, testing the mettle of the characters' emotions, calibrating the all-round credentials of love-seekers and, finally, rewarding them with much desired true love. Whatever the fate of true lovebirds, the readers are bound to enjoy the waves of emotions.

The sequel of 'JUUHHHUUUU' is in the making, exploring genres other than love.

JUUHHHUUUU

PROLOGUE

Hiii Lovely People!

Juuhhhuuuu... Juuhhhuuuu... Juuhhhuuuu...

Nowadays, thalassophiles, in this part of the world, often come across listening to this echoing word, rhyming strangely.

'Juuhhhuuuu', this word looks different, sounds different, you might have never even heard of it, or you may guess that it resembles the famous name 'Juhu' as in Juhu Beach, in Mumbai.

Yes, you are right.

But then, you might be thinking, is there any connection between 'Juuhhhuuuu' and 'Juhu'?

Yes, you are right again.

But then, what is the connection? What exactly is 'Juuhhhuuuu'? Who is 'Juuhhhuuuu'?

Hmmm... To know that, you need to have some patience. You need to visit Juhu Beach with your eyes & ears open like an emotional love-seeker, spying on the lovely beach in search of hidden love treasures.

No, no, no. It is not your classic mystery, suspense, thrill, and adventure. Rather it's more intriguing, more goosebumpy, more tickly, more awakening, more cuddling, more pampering, and last but not least, more entertaining.

But, I can't leave you whiling helplessly. So, let me give some clues. Actually, more than clues, let me give you the background of 'Juuhhhuuuu'.

Many years ago, one fine day, echoes of a child's cries surprised the early morning walkers at Juhu Beach.

They listened more attentively and moved toward the direction of the voice coming from the farthest end. When they got very close to the spot, they were shocked to find that the cries were spurting out of a sand art pyramid. Generally, artists make sand sculptures of great legends, famous themes and social messages. But surprisingly, for the first time ever, people saw a pyramid.

On a closer look, they noticed a baby, hardly a few hours old, crying badly inside the pyramid. Everyone was shocked to see the baby emotionlessly dumped at a beach, where the waves could have swept away the baby anytime or might have buried it under the ruined pyramid. But, maybe the baby's destiny could have saved it from the cruel clutches of death.

Nonetheless, how cruel the biological parents could have been to dump their child right after giving birth to it. Well, such an incident was not happening for the first time. Historically, many cases of honour abandoning a newborn have been observed.

The gathered people decided to inform the Juhu police, who immediately came into action, seized the abandoned baby and started the process of investigation.

Meanwhile, the police noticed one peculiar thing about the baby boy. His head was of conical shape. Narrower at the top and broader at the bottom, just like a pyramid. And, he was kept inside a pyramid sand art, which was not there the previous night. So, the police suspected that because of the weird shape of the skull, his parents might have executed the construction of the pyramid and dumping of the baby in the late night hours.

The police utilized their sniffer dog squad to trace the wrong-doers. They investigated the CCTV records of nearby buildings, but nothing significant was found. They performed exhaustive research on expert sand artists and records of babies born within the last 48 hours.

After a few days of investigations, when no concrete and convincing findings were in place, the police decided to give up the baby boy to Juhu Orphan House for adoption.

Chana Babu, nobody knows his real name, is a well-known Chana Jor Garam vendor at Juhu Beach. He, after coming to know about the baby, approached the police with a request to adopt that abandoned child. Chana Babu and his wife were married for 22 years but had not been blessed with a child. Being a very old and popular vendor at Juhu Beach, the police knew him well. It didn't take much time for the police to complete the legal formalities. Chana Babu and his wife graciously accepted the baby.

There were several peculiarities of the baby boy—firstly, abandoning him inside a sand pyramid at Juhu Beach; secondly, the pyramid-shaped head; thirdly, the untraceability of the biological parents despite using advanced technologies; and fourthly, his being adopted by Juhu Beach inhabitants. Nonetheless, the couple was very happy with this blessing in disguise.

After a few days, when the time came for the naming ceremony, Chana Babu settled for a very peculiar name. The name echoing the story of his birth circumstances and the shape of his head.

Yeah! You guessed it right. PYRAMID...

Later, the boy became a famous personality at Juhu Beach, not only because of the mystery surrounding his birth, the shape of his head, and his name but for many other surprising things.

Chana Babu and his wife, Chana Bhabhi, brought up Pyramid with the sweetest pampering mixed with great care for his all-round growth in education, sports, music, arts, and many multidisciplinary skills. They provided him with the best facilities they could afford. Apart from schooling hours, Chana Babu used to keep Pyramid with him. He would train him for his business of selling Chana Jor Garam at Juhu Beach by reciting spontaneous funny poetries. Sometimes, Pyramid would sell snacks with Chana Bhabhi. Apart from selling snacks, the Chana couple used to encourage him to do various other activities, too. Like wave surfing, cricket, gymnastics, football, basketball, etc.

After a few years, though circumstances forced him to discontinue education after higher secondary, he was still the loving son of his proud ageing parents. Chana Babu and Chana Bhabhi did not remain as active in their business as they were, so Pyramid took over and continued the legacy.

Pyramid had developed a few surprising skills. Thanks to the foreign tourists, now he was an expert at speaking many foreign languages with proper accents: American English, British English, German, Italian, Spanish, Russian, Chinese, Japanese, Nigerian, Urdu, Arabic, and many more. He also developed the great art of storytelling. The stories that he came to know from various resources, like police, lovers on the beach, foreign tourists, and his own experiences. However, the real-life stories that happened at

Juhu Beach fascinated him more. So, whenever he happened to be in an artistic mood, he would put his business on hold and enjoy himself as a hearty storyteller to small crowds of admirers of him.

One evening, after suffering a marriage proposal rejection at his home, he returned to Juhu Beach and started boozing with a few close friends. That evening he was so upset that he didn't return home despite his parents' continuous requests on calls. He continued drinking even after all his friends left one-after-another. Having good relations with the police was why he was allowed to continue drinking at a secret spot on the beach.

He couldn't remember when he fell asleep. But, when he woke up, the moon was smiling and the sun hadn't arisen. He couldn't know the time as his mobile's battery was drained off, and he was lying heavily intoxicated on the deserted beach.

With blurry eyes, he saw a peculiar creature lying over his lap. Amid a heavy hangover, at first glance, he couldn't understand anything and pushed the creature off his body. But, when he heard a squeaky voice like that of a bird, he felt sorry. He struggled to sit up at the spot and slowly slid towards that creature. When he looked closer, he found that it was a bird, crying with its eyes closed.

As his vision cleared, he looked around and found a few half-empty water bottles lying around. First, he washed his face and eyes and then came back to the bird. Now, he recognized that it was a new born parrot. It was still squeaking. He felt guilty for throwing it away.

So, he poured a little water into the bird's mouth and then started comforting it by softly massaging its body. After a few minutes, when baby parrot seemed comfortable, but its eyes were still closed.

The parrot was very beautiful with rainbow-coloured wings. In fact, his whole body—eyes, chest, beak, feet, and rump—was full of various pleasant colours. Surprisingly, even its size was abnormally bigger than normal baby parrots.

Nonetheless, after seeing it, Pyramid's hangover disappeared. The upsetting pain of the previous day's rejection was also quickly fading away from his memories.

Pyramid felt positive and thought that the day had started with a blessed gift.

He hurried towards his home to surprise his parents. When Chana Babu and Chana Bhabhi saw the parrot, they couldn't control their outburst of love for that beautiful bird. Chana Bhabhi gave a bath to the baby parrot and fed it milk. After that, it soon fell asleep.

At the very first glance itself, they decided to adopt this baby parrot. So, they started having brain storming discussions.

"The parrot seems to be of foreign breed, as it is bigger with multiple colours, very much different from the Indian breeds."

"How did it reach Juhu Beach, and that too on the laps of sleeping Pyramid? Did its parents dump it there intentionally or did it get separated from its parents? Or did a trafficker dump it there? But, how could a baby survive in such tough conditions."

There were a lot of questions about the parrot, but they remained unanswered. Partly satisfying answers were found about its breed, which part of the world it belonged to, etc. Finally, the discussions remained unconcluded as various properties it had were common to many other breeds.

They didn't bother too much about those General Knowledge questions and devoted their time to bringing up the bird like their own baby.

Meanwhile, one thing about the parrot was bothering them. Since the beginning, the parrot was suffering from a cold and throat infection.

They guessed that it was because of the extreme cold conditions at the beach. Pyramid consulted a vet to get the parrot treated.

As a few months passed, the cough and cold subsided. But, there was no satisfactory improvement in the throat infection. The doctor advised Pyramid to start training the parrot to speak, which might heal the sore throat.

Pyramid started training it to speak and sing like a human. Not only speaking but imitating other people in both male and female voices. When Pyramid started training it to speak 'Juhu', which was his own favourite word, then maybe out of its sore throat or childishness or animal instincts, it would speak the word in a stammering voice, "Juuhhhuuuu," with a peculiar parroty rhythm, which surprisingly always pleased Pyramid despite sounding awkward.

For a few more days, Pyramid tried his level best to train the parrot to speak 'Juhu' correctly, but all efforts went in vain. The parrot always stammered and pronounced it 'Juuhhhuuuu'.

Finally, Pyramid concluded to accept that peculiar pronunciation, which was grammatically wrong but sounded pleasant and garnered attention.

That's why comical Pyramid named his parrot friend 'Juuhhhuuuu'.

At Juhu Beach, now the visitors often came across the recitals of 'Juuhhhuuuu'.

So, that's the story behind the word, the name, 'Juuhhhuuuu'.

Later on, Pyramid trained it to memorize and speak long stories, songs and poetries. Except for 'JUHU', the parrot learnt to pronounce every word very much correctly.

Time went by as usual.

Then after a few years, the baby parrot grew into an adult parrot. Very big in size, approx. 3'6" and gloriously colourful. It was a delightful pleasure to watch. More than that, this parrot was trained as a multi-skill performer.

Last but not least, I am Juuhhhuuuu, the parrot friend of Pyramid. Always with him, selling Chana Jor Garam at Juhu Beach. And, whenever my mood swings, I fly across Juhu Beach.

Many lovely people who visit here come to meet me and sometimes listen to my stories. Though generally, Pyramid tells the stories, sometimes he asks me to narrate the stories.

Now, for all of you lovely people, we are bringing a few stories that happened in and around Juhu Beach and other parts of the world. I am sure, you will find that all those stories are the rarest of rare kinds of stories.

So, dear, enjoy the stories.

See you around Juhu Beach. Bye!

Please don't forget to tell your friends about me. Post your valuable reviews and like me on social media and purchase platforms.

JUUHHHUUUU

Hi Fellas!

So, today, I am going to tell you a uniquely strange story that happened at Juhu Beach.

This story was told to me by Pyramid on Valentine's Day this year.

In one line, this story is about "The strange consequences of an accident at Juhu Beach".

***

Chapter 1

ACCIDENTED SOULS

Evergreen Juhu Beach, Mumbai

Awesome August

Saturday, Naughty Noon Hour

There was a very thin crowd at Juhu Beach, at the noon hour, on a sensual windy day with intermittent titillating drizzles, sometimes greyish cloudy and sometimes satiny shiny. Sultry waves kept on kissing the velvety sand and, on the other side, endlessly tried to hug the flirty sky.

A group of lovely ladies from nearby societies, in modern casuals, were enjoying an umbrella-less monsoon walk, were chatting near the mysterious Mermaid Statue. Nobody could guess that all working women turned homemakers were in their late forties, credit to womanlier hacks. Still full of adolescent girly carefree traits at bottom of their hearts.

Pyari, blissfully twirling while holding her drenched silky hairs embedded with her favourite pink rose buds, said, "Wow! Really, really, really enjoyed this walk! Isn't it mommy girls?"

Pavitra reverted, "Ya, true. But got wet, yaar. All clothes are flimsy."

Chanchal giggled with a naughty smile. "Ya, baby, it's visible. But no hungry brat is there to watch that. Haha."

"Yes, but, now I am feeling hungry. I can even eat a horse," Belle said, drumming over her belly.

Sahiba suggested bossily, "Ok! Let's go to TAP Hotel, in front of us."

"No, yaar! Let's go to our favourite food stall," Meena said.

Sahiba objected, "But, dear! It's monsoon season. Food stalls are not hygienic."

Meena sarcastically said, "Are you hygienic, babe?"

Sahiba got irritated. "Oh! What the hell are you talking about? I said TAP for our safety only."

"Decide fast!" Pyari urged.

Chanchal giggled again. "Why fast. Why in so much hurry, yaar? The children and husband will be coming home in the evening only... Oh sorry, you don't even have to bother about children! Is anybody else to do anything else?"

"Mind your tongue! Why do you often pinch Pyari for not having children?" Meena softly slammed.

Pyari reasoned, "Are Baba! Calm down. Calm down. Actually, I have to go to the washroom, that's why."

Pavitra was feeling uncomfortable in wet clothes and with childish chats. "How long will we stand here? Let's go to food stalls."

Sahiba passively surrendered. "Ok! Let's move, but I hate street food!"

Meena taunted, "It's not a street, babe! It's a beach! Better than a million streets."

Sahiba shook her head, avoiding eye contact. "LOL! By the way, that might be better for Pavitra, who is scared of poopy-eyed stray fellas."

The ladies started moving toward food stalls.

Pyari yelled while turning towards the beach washroom, "Ok! I will be joining soon."

*

A few minutes later, after relieving herself, Pyari stood near the mermaid statue, about to turn toward the food stalls, when suddenly her mobile rang.

She took out her waterproof mobile and responded to Sahiba. "Hello! What happened?"

Sahiba said with proud sarcasm, "Babe! At last, I won. Come to TAP. We are here only."

Pyari smiled. "Oh! Congrats! What a roller coaster! Ok, I am just coming in two minutes."

Sahiba said in a winner's voice, "Ya babe! Rain *Rani* helped me win. Come fast."

By that time, suddenly the drizzle thickened with an intense downpour and loud thundering. Clouds changed their colours from pale grey to dark grey, winds geared up, and visibility also faded slightly.

Standing below the mermaid statue, Pyari looked around, finding traffic—not so bothersome—and feeling the thumping heavy raindrops. She decided to run across the one-way road, which had a wide divider.

Sensing the opportune moment, Pyari ran towards TAP. She jumped over the divider and moved ahead, but suddenly a screech followed her from her left. A screeching sound coupled with honking echoed around that area and suddenly a scary hard-hitting sound echoed. A scooty rammed into her. Her body tumbled and then rolled around a few times on the road. She struck the pedestrian walkway with a bang, blood spilling from her head, flowing into the drainage and mixing with the rainwater. All embedded roses too splattered around and mixed in the pool of blood and rainwater. The scooty skidded and wobbled after smashing Pyari, but the lady riding it seemed to be a good driver as she controlled it quickly, glimpsed back, didn't stop and drove away.

Amidst the intense downpour, a few pedestrians, TAP's security guard and even people from the corresponding traffic lane reached out to help. Nobody could see the face of the lady on the scooty as she was wearing a raincoat and helmet.

However, for a few, the presence of mind kicked in, and they clicked pictures and shot videos as soon as they heard the sound of the crash. The vehicle no. of the scooty was recorded. Even CCTV Cameras installed there captured the whole incident.

As soon as the rain halted, the TAP security guard recognized Pyari, as he had seen those ladies chatting near the mermaid statue and then all the ladies except Pyari checked into the Hotel just a few minutes back.

The security guard ran inside, informed the manager, and then the manager immediately informed Pyari's friends about the incident. Shocked, all the ladies rushed outside and found bleeding Pyari lying over the footpath, surrounded by a few good souls trying to help her.

That's the spirit of Juhu Beach and this magical city. Mumbaikars just rush in selflessly to help the needy.

The playful mommy girls, trembled when they saw the deadly scene. They screamed louder & louder and burst into tears. Meanwhile, the hotel manager called up for an ambulance and sent the security guard to the Juhu Beach Police Station to inform the police about the accident.

Meanwhile, all uncontrollably sobbing friends appeared to be in a similar emotional trauma. Pavitra forgot about the visibility of her drenched clothes; Chanchal was no more giggling; Belle lost her hunger; Sahiba was not bossy anymore and Meena forgot about the latest gossip.

The police jumped into action and enquired a couple of people in the crowd who shared pictures and videos of the incident. The police investigation process started quickly in association with the traffic police. Meanwhile, Super Speciality Cardio Ambulance reached there and unconscious Pyari was on her way to nearby Juhu Star Hospital, at the junction of ST Road & Juhu Road. Her friends followed with the help of the police.

While on the way to the hospital, Police Inspector, Juhi Shinde got an update about the lady riding the scooty. He instructed a team to catch the culprit.

A few minutes later at the hospital, as the doctor was performing the preliminary check-up, he declared Pyari dead. He requested Inspector and her friends to inform her family and furnish the necessary details before handing over the body.

What a cruel twist of incidences, the exhilarating drizzle walk ending in doomed mourning.

*

Pyari's lamenting friends were consoling each other. They called their husbands, briefed them about the unfortunate incident, and asked them to come immediately to the hospital. Meanwhile, Juhi Shinde got the contact details of Jeet, Pyari's husband, from her friends and informed him about the incident, requesting him to come to the hospital as early as possible.

The shocking news of Pyari's untimely demise out of an unfortunate accident, affected Jeet so deeply that his blood pressure rose. With shaking hands and trembling legs, drowned in saddened thoughts, he lit a cigarette. He didn't even bother to inform anybody in his office as he limpingly moved to his BMW and dashed to reach the hospital.

Jeet, a self-made man, was a middle-aged property consultant, running a business from his office located in Santacruz. His business was running very well, as he was a channel partner of many top-brass Builders & Developers. Often busy in business, he couldn't devote much time to his wife. The couple was not very worried about not having children even at this age. Often people found him humble, a sweet talker, having sharp business acumen with an approach of due diligence, a man of commitment and a loyal friend. Never ever anybody saw him as arrogant, wild or engaged in any misconduct.

Meanwhile, a police team reached MSB Bank, Juhu Road, to catch the culprit. The Bank Manager was shocked when police inquired about a staff named Jasmine. She couldn't sustain the investigations for long, broke down and confessed the wrongdoing.

Actually, it was the marriage anniversary of Jasmine & her husband, Dev. She wanted to surprise her husband with an imported gift she ordered through courier. Around noon, she got a call from the courier delivery boy who asserted that it was the third attempt at delivering the package, and if she didn't collect it now she would have to get it from their office. And after a week, it would be sent back to the sender if not collected from the office. The parcel being valuable wasn't to be delivered to anyone but the registered receiver.

So, in that emergency situation, Jasmine requested an hour off from her office to receive the package. As it was a rainy day, she wore the rain coat and had a helmet securing her head. Jasmine, known to be a scooty racer among her friends, left in a hurry because, within an hour, she had to manage to reach home, receive the courier, and then return to Bank, that too in such weather, riding over slippery roads.

Just as she crossed the Bora Bora Hotel and was about to turn into the other end of the 'S' curve turning, amid the instant downpour and fading visibility, she saw a lady hurriedly crossing the road from the beachside. Jasmine tried to apply the brakes, but couldn't manage to halt the scooty. The scooty hit the lady and then started wobbling but, somehow, Jasmine controlled it. She glimpsed back and drove away.

"Why didn't you stop there to help that lady?" Juhi Shinde asked Jasmine.

"I was scared that I wouldn't be able to handle the shock of an accident, and I was in a great hurry also," Jasmine sobbingly responded.

"We understand, you got scared, and didn't even inform your office. But, did you inform your husband?"

"No, I was scared to even inform him. I thought I will tell him later," Jasmine whispered still sobbing.

"Let's go to the parking. We want to check your scooty."

"Scooty is not here. I put it in a nearby garage because its front panel and front indicator were damaged."

"Then how did you return?"

"Taxi."

"Good, very good, Madam! You are still playing around. Before returning, you thought that you and your scooty could be recognized by people. That's why you put it in a garage and came back by taxi," Juhi Shinde accused. "We will check the condition of your scooty. What's the name of that garage?"

"Uhhh," Jasmine mumbled.

"What uhhh?" Juhi Shinde was getting irritated.

"Ah... It's Amar Garage, near my house in Santacruz," Jasmine managed to say.

"Why did it take so long?" she asked suspiciously. Then she turned and told a constable, "Patil, go right now and check the Amar Garage."

Jasmine's eyebrows shrunk without disturbing other facial expressions and her sobbing.

Juhi Shinde again turned to Jasmine. "So, at the accident location, what did you see while returning?"

"I didn't see anything," Jasmine responded with more confidence and hope in her eyes.

"So, what did you think at that time?"

"I thought nothing went wrong and that lady might not have hurt as badly as it seemed while I glimpsed."

"So, what did you feel that time?"

"I felt relieved and happy, too, as there was nothing serious to worry about that accident." This time Jasmine smiled slightly.

"Oh! How judgmental you are, Madam! Do you know what happened to that lady?"

"No! Because..."

"That lady lost her life, a few minutes back. Her body is lying in Juhu Star Hospital, and her husband will be reaching there in a few minutes." Juhi Shinde came to the point. "Waghmare, Jasmine Madam is not cooperating fairly. Call her husband."

Constable Waghmare called Dev and asked him to come to his wife's office for some urgent issue. When asked what was it about, the constable rudely spoke, "Will let know once you reach here."

Dev was an IT Manager in a multinational firm located in Santacruz. It was their 20th marriage anniversary and, unfortunately, that sad incident happened, where Jasmine could be charged with a hit & run case, accidental killing and a few more.

While being interrogated, initially, she denied everything, but when the pictures, videos and CCTV footage were shown to her, she changed the track.

After getting the call from the police, Dev suddenly got highly tensed. Drowned in thoughts of worst-case scenarios, he lit a cigarette. He called off the day at his office and hurried towards his sports bike and dashed to reach MSB Bank.

At the bank, Juhi Shinde continued interrogating Jasmine. However, after some time she got irritated because of Jasmine's misleading responses and asked the constable for an update on her husband.

Constable Waghmare, after contacting Jasmine's husband, updated Inspector Shinde that within ten minutes he will be reaching.

*

The saddened husband, Jeet, despite the rainy weather, slippery roads, and poor visibility, in order to reach the hospital at the earliest, was driving rashly, bothering other vehicles around.

After some time, when he touched the Juhu Beach area, crossing the Bora Bora Hotel, and was about to turn into the other end of the 'S' curve turning, amid the instant downpour and fading visibility, he saw a biker struggling with a few freely lying Road Divider Barricades. Jeet tried to apply the brakes, but couldn't manage to halt the car. The screeching sound coupled with honking echoed around that area and suddenly a scary hard-hitting sound echoed. Jeet's car rammed into the biker. The biker's body, along with the bike, tumbled a few feet high and fell a few feet away. His body rolled around a few times on the road and struck the pedestrian walkway with a bang, blood spilling from his head. The car skidded and wobbled, but Jeet controlled it quickly, glimpsed back, decided to return later, and drove away.

A few travellers and drivers stopped in shock but many didn't bother and rode away. For a few, the presence of mind kicked in, and they clicked pictures and shot videos as soon as they heard the sound of the crash. The vehicle no. of the car was recorded. Even CCTV Cameras installed there captured the whole incident.

Someone called up an ambulance and the police. Juhu Police team quickly reached over there and coordinated with the traffic police for the CCTV footage to locate the car and the owner's details. They enquired a couple of people in the crowd who shared pictures and videos of the incident. As informed by the pedestrians, the information of the car's further movement was shared with the traffic police to catch the hit-and-run accused driver. Meanwhile, Super Speciality Cardio Ambulance reached there and the unconscious biker was on his way to nearby Juhu Star Hospital, at the junction of ST Road & Juhu Road.

Already saddened by his wife's death and now panicked by the accident, Jeet managed to reach Juhu Star Hospital. When Jeet saw the silenced lifeless face of his wife, he broke down into heart-wrenching cries. Pyari's friends tried to comfort him, but he sobbed uncontrollably. The hospital staff and Pyari's friends understood his emotions and preferred to wait for him to calm down.

*

Inspector Juhi Shinde got fed up while waiting for Jasmine's husband and again asked Constable Waghmare to contact Dev.

Waghmare tried a couple of times, but Dev's mobile was switched off.

"Like wife, like husband. Absconding, fearing to face the police... Hopeless," roared Juhi Shinde and instructed Waghmare to inform Dev to come directly to Juhu Police Station and moved there with Jasmine in custody.

*

Meanwhile, the police got the details of the car and its owner involved in the hit-and-run case. To their surprise, it was Jeet. The police tried contacting him, but the call was not being attended to as he was still deep into mourning. However, when the mobile kept on ringing, he handed it over to Meena who was standing close to him.

Meena without any prejudices told the police about the whereabouts of Jeet.

The police reached the hospital soon. Just before they could approach him, the conversation between the hospital staff and Pyari's friends hinted at the demise of Pyari, Jeet's wife. However, they couldn't wait anymore.

"Mr Jeet, sorry for your loss, but we need to talk to you. If possible...please," Sub-Inspector Deshmukh asserted.

Wiping his tears, controlling and pushing down his emotions, Jeet responded positively. "Yes, Sir! Please tell me."

"Not here. Let's move into Doctor's cabin"

Though Jeet controlled his emotions sensibly during the interrogation, Jeet didn't take much time confessing what had happened.

Soon, Sub-Inspector Deshmukh requested the Doctor In-charge to keep the dead body in their custody till further instructions from the police. He then arrested Jeet and escorted him to the Juhu Police Station, leaving behind Pyari's friends in dilemma.

By the time the second team led by Sub-Inspector Deshmukh reached Juhu Police Station, the first team led by Inspector Juhi Shinde had just finished registering an FIR against Jasmine. Juhi Shinde asked Jasmine to wait in the small waiting lobby reserved for the accused, duly watched by gunned police guards. Within a couple of hours, when the process for FIR was completed for Jeet, he also was asked to wait in the same lobby.

Deeply disturbed Jeet, felt uncomfortable when he saw a lady already sitting there. Though she was looking damn pretty, emotionally broken Jeet was not in the mood to have any interaction with her. At that point, only the two accused were sitting and waiting for a further course of action. At such an intense, odd moment, Jasmine couldn't stay quiet and broke the irritating silence.

"Hi. Why have they brought you here?" Jasmine inquired innocently in a soft, sweet voice.

Jeet just gazed at her. He couldn't speak a word. He took out his handkerchief to wipe his teary eyes, but it fell on the floor.

Jasmine, showing courtesy, got up from the bench, picked up the handkerchief, and helped him wipe his face and eyes. After a few moments, when she sensed that the guy is settled, she tried to dig for information. "So, what brought you here?"

"I got a call from the police. They found a dead body. It was kept in Juhu Star Hospital. It seemed to resemble my wife. So, they requested me to come down to identify it. But, while coming to the hospital, I met with an accident on Juhu Beach road and hit a biker. Unfortunately, that biker died. So, a hit-and-run case is filed against me," he said with a choked throat.

"Oh! Very sad! Sorry for your loss. Sorry for that biker also."

"Suddenly, life has crumbled into pieces. Why? Why did it happen to me? I never did any wrong to anybody. Don't know for which sins I am being punished?"

"Don't worry! Mata Rani's blessings are with you."

"And, what brought you here?" Jeet inquisitively asked.

"Oh! Mine is also somewhat... a similar case," Jasmine fumbled hesitantly.

"Means?" Jeet curiously asked as he noticed her fumbling.

"Means, I also met with an accident. I was on a scooty and hit a lady who was wrongly crossing the road. Don't know, how these buggers found me and arrested me for no mistake of mine."

"Oh! Very sad! Did anybody from family or friends come to see you here?"

"Ya, my husband is coming."

Jeet smelled something shady about the lady, but he didn't pursue the matter further. Since the last few hours had been mentally and emotionally exhausting, he took out his cigarette packet and lit one. Jasmine glimpsed at him and gestured requesting a cigarette.

He offered her one and helped her light it.

"I tried to quit many times but," Jeet was trying to speak when a lady constable came in.

She grunted authoritatively, "Mrs Jasmine! Come. Sir is calling."

Jasmine smiled while smoking threw away the cigarette butt carelessly, got up, and immediately moved behind the lady constable.

Before crossing the lobby gate, a familiar voice followed her. "It's Jeet."

She halfheartedly turned slightly and mumbled. "Nice meeting. Bye."

Amid life's turbulent heartbreaking moments, meeting such a beautiful, quirky, glib storyteller lady with magical deluding eyes brought a soothing diversion to Jeet's suppressed emotions, even though she was just the opposite of his beloved Pyari's innocent persona.

After a couple of hours, Jeet was called up and informed that he was being taken into police remand for two days and he would have to appear in Magistrate Court after that for the scheduled hearing. When he requested bail with the help of his advocate, he was handed over his phone and allowed to only contact his advocate.

After a couple of hours, his advocate came there and informed him that it was Saturday and bail was not possible. They would have to face the court hearing on Monday. The advocate was confident that he would get bail on Monday.

After the meeting, Jeet was guided by a constable and moved into the lock-up room of Juhu Police Station.

Upset Jeet didn't look around. He just sank to the floor of the lockup cell amid the bombardments of negativities out of his painful emotions. Within a few hours, the life fractured into unrepairable pieces. Amid tears and emotional turbulences, sudden sobbing noises distracted him. When he looked around, he found a lady sitting on the floor of the adjoining lockup cell. Her face was covered with a scarf and her head was on her knees. Despite his own pain, he felt sympathy towards that woman.

Out of curiosity, he whispered, "Hello! Excuse me! Can I..."

Words echoed, breaking the sobbing spree. The lady raised her head and turned in the direction of the voice.

Seeing each other, they both uttered in chorus, "You!"

"But, your husband was coming to help you out. What happened?" Jeet asked inquisitively.

"No. Soon after they brought me here, they told me that as my husband was coming to meet me, he met with an accident and died on the spot." She bawled in pain. "The lady who was hit by my scooty also died. Now, I am being arrested. On Monday, I will be presented in court."

"Oh! That's very sad. Sorry for your loss. When will they take you to see him...his body?" sympathized Jeet.

"Don't know. I asked, but they said they would let me know very soon." Jasmine kept on sobbing, intermittently looking at him.

"Any relatives, friends who can help you?" asked Jeet.

"No. Nobody knows about all this. My mobile is with the police. Even people from my office did not approach the police afterwards. I don't know what will happen. My life is completely spoiled."

"Yes, bad time for good people like us. But, don't lose hope. On Monday, I will talk to my lawyer to take up your case too"

"Hmm... Really, you are too good. In these heartbreaking moments of life, you came as a God to me. I am really thankful." Jasmine opened her heart to him.

"We must help each other. That's what I believe."

Meanwhile, a constable brought food packets for them for dinner.

After they had it, they kept on talking the whole night. The wounds and pain they had suffered that day, stole away their sleep.

*

Sunday

Juhu Police Station

The next day, the police escorted Jasmine to Juhu Star Hospital to identify the dead body of her husband, Dev. There, Jasmine broke down on seeing her husband lying in the mortuary with just a tag on his toe.

When she calmed down, the police got the contact details of her relatives and friends and arranged to call them for further inquiry and legal requirements.

Since Dev couldn't update the police that he was going to see his wife, Inspector Juhi Shinde suspected him of absconding. She rigorously tried to locate him by tracking his mobile, but as it was switched off, the IT Cell was involved in locating his mobile, and it took time. It was only in the late night hours that they got his location and came to know about the accident.

Inspector instructed the hospital to keep the dead bodies with them until further notice.

Meanwhile, Pyari's friends and their spouses visited Juhu Police Station and requested a meeting with Jeet. But, they were not allowed and a guard advised them to meet him in court on Monday. Jeet's friends, relatives and colleagues also visited but received the same response.

After returning from the hospital, Jasmine shared the sad news with Jeet. They both spent the time comforting each other amid intermittent sobs and tears.

In those moments in the lock-up, it never seemed that they were strangers to each other. Instead, felt like long-time buddies, caring for and comforting each other during the saddest moments of their life.

*

Monday

Magistrate Court

Police escorted Jeet and Jasmine separately to court.

Meanwhile, before the trials began, Jeet request his lawyer to provide legal services to Jasmine too.

Jasmine felt a little comfortable when she saw her parents, Dev's family and a few close relatives and friends. She felt better when she came to know that a lawyer had been arranged for her.

The first call was made for Jasmine's hit-and-run case.

Jasmine bluntly denied all the accusations made by the prosecutor and blamed the poor deceased for the consequences that occurred who, in heavy rain and low visibility, violated the traffic signal and was wrongly crossing the road despite her honking. It caused the collision and, in turn, led to the victim's death.

Jasmine's statements annoyed Pyari's friends, relatives and family members present in the court but pleased her own lawyer, family members and friends.

Witnesses present at the time of the accident were also presented to the court for their testimony.

After some time, Jeet was brought into the witness box as the husband of the deceased. Jasmine couldn't control her emotions. She was shocked, and she broke down. She started crying and screamed out in guilt in the crowded courtroom. For the last two days in the lockup, she had developed strong feelings for him, because of his nobility and kind nature. She couldn't stop cursing herself for the damage she unintentionally caused to him, for being the reason for his beloved wife's untimely death.

However, she still didn't bother to accept the accusations out of her self-centred mindset.

Jeet's mask was unveiled too. When he came to know that Jasmine was the killer of his wife his reactions were too quirky. In tears, he openly cursed her for killing his wife. He lambasted Jasmine for her tricky lies and pseudo-behavioural traits.

Surprisingly, his reactions didn't seem to hurt Jasmine. She felt that she would have reacted similarly if she were in his shoes.

After reviewing all inputs submitted by the prosecutor and hearing the plea from the accused and testaments from the witnesses, the judge ordered to submit a detailed investigation report of the accident with micro details of weather conditions including visibility scale, the live traffic signal report and the facts about honking activity to evaluate the incident by recreating the actual scenario and considering Jasmine's credentials of last 10 years from MSB Bank.

Jasmine was escorted out to a nearby waiting room. Her lawyer, family and friends followed her.

"Now my hearing is done... I mean would I be taken back?" irritated Jasmine hurriedly asked the escorting lady constable.

"Calm down. Calm down," groaned the lady constable.

Jasmine, a happy-go-lucky and self-protective middle-aged woman, was feeling so low and upset for the last two days that now everything was irritating her in the court. More so, since the deeds of Jasmine's hit-and-run case were questioned in court along with the revelation that the victim was, in fact, Jeet's wife. She was already devastated after hearing the news of the demise of her beloved husband.

After a few minutes, Jeet's hit-and-run case began with Jeet being interrogated by the prosecution.

Jeet, a fair-minded man of principles, accepted all the accusations and expressed his willingness to cooperate with the law. But, his lawyer was not happy with him for his straight confession.

After the testaments by the witnesses, the judge ordered to present the immediate family of the deceased to register the statements. As soon as Jasmine was brought into the witness box in front of Jeet and told that he was the culprit behind her husband's death, all skies fell down, all walls crumbled. Jasmine couldn't tolerate those inflammable words pouring on her like melted lava.

She screamed in her loudest voice, "Bastard!"

With a reddened face and tears in her eyes, she jumped out of the witness box, wildly rushed into Jeet's witness box and went insanely violent. She grabbed his collar with one hand, threw punches at his chest with the other hand, and kicked him with her legs.

"Bastard! Murderer! You killed my husband. You spoiled my life." Jasmine lambasted Jeet with her words as well as with punches and kicks.

Jeet was trying to safeguard himself by small movements back and forth.

Everybody was stunned including Jasmine's family and lawyer. The security guards and escort police teams rushed toward them to control the chaos.

"Order, order, order," the Judge yelled, thumping his hammer on his desk.

Police guards rushed in and rescued Jeet from Jasmine's assault, and lady police guards dragged Jasmine toward the other witness box.

Jasmine kept on shouting and crying. "Rascal! Shows off that he is so decent. But, he actually stabbed in the back. He killed my innocent husband."

"Order, order, order,", repeated the Judge

"Judge Sahab, hang him. Hang him. He spoiled my life."

"Madam! This is court, not your house. Control yourself and maintain the decorum of the court. The law doesn't work on emotions, the law works on facts and evidence. The court warns you not to repeat such an unruly act, else strict action will be taken against you," the Judge roared authoritatively.

Hearing that, Jasmine realized that she lost control over her emotions and tried to cool down. She kept crying, though now in a low voice.

Jasmine's melodrama shocked everybody around. Her parents knew of her erratic mood swings but had never seen her throwing such violent tantrums. On one hand, a few minutes ago, she was sympathizing with Jeet after knowing the fact that she was the culprit of his wife's death, whereas, on the other hand, she shed off all those sympathies, abused him and didn't even hesitate to physically attack him in the court after knowing that Jeet was responsible for her husband's death.

Jeet didn't feel much upset because, a few minutes back, he had also reacted in a similar manner.

*

The interesting thing that happened throughout the prosecution process was how smartly the police handled the overall legal process of the twin cases, strangely linked to each other.

On the day of the accident, late at night, after compiling all the facts and figures, when Juhu Police Station In-Charge was reviewing the reports with the respective case leaders, he was surprised to see the strange coincidences of the two hit-and-run cases where both the accused were guilty of accidentally killing each other's spouses.

To avoid the unnecessary drama in the lock-up, the police strategically preferred not to reveal the strangely troubling truth to either of the prisoners. They cleverly pushed the climax of the cruel truth to the prosecution process of the honourable court.

Finally, the judge declared the decision for the proceedings. Jasmine & Jeet were sent to judicial custody, and the next hearing date was scheduled after 30 days.

In jail, they were kept in separate cells and never ever got any opportunity to even see each other.

*

Time never stops...

Here also, hearings over hearings continued in the court for a couple of months. Everyone's patience limits seemed to be exhausted with the announcement for every next hearing

Though the prosecution for the accidental killing against Jeet was absolutely clear because of his confession, his urge to minimize the punishment was prolonging the case.

As far as Jasmine's case was concerned, her continued adamant denials in response to the accusations made the case much more complicated. In every hearing, her statements consistently accused Pyari's careless road-crossing for the accident, and, in turn, her unfortunate death. The unclear noises and poor visibility conditions at the time of the accident diluted the relevance of the evidence. Though Jasmine was always in denial, she had no honest response to the accusations.

Her lack of cooperation led to Narco Test and Brain Mapping, but even then nothing concrete came up.

Meanwhile, both Jeet and Jasmine were continuously trying to get bail from the judiciary, but all efforts went in vain.

After more than half a year, the court finally passed the verdict. Jasmine and Jeet both were penalized with two years of rigorous imprisonment and five lakh rupees as a penalty. In Jasmine's case, Pyari was adjudged to get the benefit of the doubt.

Not satisfied with the verdict, they both appealed to the High Court.

Again, the cycle of multiple hearings went on for a few months.

The High Court Judge, in one such hearing, responded in an unexpected manner. "Listen, the law is not for punishing the culprit but to provide justice to the victim and their families. In this unique case, both the accused are mutual culprits and mutual victims. These two are the rarest of the rare cases, which could be amicably concluded beyond the books without disturbing the due diligence of law."

Jasmine's Lawyer interrupted, "My Lord! What do you mean to say"

"Let me finish first!"

Jasmine's advocate nodded his head.

"See, Jasmine and Jeet both were convicted by the Magistrate Court for accidental killing, surprisingly, the victims were each other's spouses, resulting in an untimely loss of their lives. Now, losing a spouse at such a middle age has already been a big tragic blow to both of their lives, even if somebody else's wrongdoing was responsible for that.

Now, we need to think whether for the sake of justice towards the deceased punishing the deceased's spouse with two years imprisonment will be righteous. Will it restore the life of the deceased's spouse to normal?

So, the question arises, can we avoid further damage to the life of the deceased's spouse? Is there any solution to restore their ruined life? Because whatever happened was out of unintentional human errors. And here, in these cases, both the convicts mutually share the sufferings and guilts of the same amount.

So, it's my advice to the convicts and their respective lawyers to undergo well-guided counselling, duly supported by the court and find a mutually agreeable solution for an out-of-the-court settlement. In my opinion, that will be the best judgement we can reward the departed souls.

And then the court was adjourned.

*

In the array of painful twists and turns, that was the most adorable twist in the lives of Jasmine and Jeet, which showered bright hopes into their deserted life.

So, under the mediatorship of the counsellor appointed by the court, in the very first round of meetings, the environment was not as encouraging as it was meant to be. Jasmine's lawyer seemed to be manipulating the lifetime opportunity to extract the best possible compensation for his client. Whereas, Jeet and his lawyer were considering that opportunity as a blessing in disguise and were ready to pay reasonable compensation to get rid of this mess. Mainly, the discussions were going on between the counsellor and the lawyers. Despite all the efforts for deriving an amicable solution, the discussions seemed to be wandering directionlessly.

Irritated by the ongoing mess, Jasmine interrupted, "What rubbish are you guys talking about? Just doing a time pass. Do you know what trauma I am passing through? I lost my husband. He was my only reason to live. Now I only have my elderly parents. I am an only child, and I lost my job. How will I survive?"

"But Mam, we are ready to pay compensation, but your lawyer asking for unreasonable..." Jeet's lawyer tried to reason.

Jasmine lost her mind on that comment. "What unreasonable? What do you mean by reasonable? Can your compensation bring back my husband? Can it give me children? We were planning for IVF. How will I live the rest of my life like a widow?"

"Same here. Same with my client. He lost his wife, and she can't be brought back. He suffered heavy losses in his business. Nobody else in the family. How will he spend his life ahead?"

Jasmine couldn't tolerate the sarcasm, lost control, stood up, and shouted, "What the hell are you talking about? He is a man, a rich man, who can marry any woman anytime. But I am a woman, a widow, a so-called criminal...a killer. Who will marry me? Who will marry me?"

"I will. I will marry you," the soft, soothing, confident words of Jeet surprised everybody around, even Jasmine.

But stunned Jasmine soon poised herself. "I don't need anybody's charity. I am not a beggar."

"It's not charity. Actually, in the moments we spent together in lockup, I liked your extroversion, archness, and straightforwardness. I liked your voice, your anger..." Jeet could keep going on and on but was interrupted by bemused Jasmine.

Jasmine blushed while remembering those moments. She whispered softly, "Do you still remember those moments?"

"Yes! How can I forget? Those feelings have been staying in my heart since. I would never have said anything, but it just came out with the flow of emotions," Jeet uttered fondly.

"Do you like me? Do you still like the lady who killed your wife?" Jasmine whispered with a choked throat.

"Neither you killed my wife nor I killed your husband. An unfortunate coincidence snatched them away from our lives. And believe me, you are still the bubbly tomboyish girl I saw that day."

"Oh, I never thought about it like this...but... but..." Jasmine got emotional, her eyes filled with tears of rare joy.

"No ifs, no buts. Now what?" Jeet intervened.

"No, no, no, Jeetji. Not like that. What I wanted to say is that I am a little bit bossy. I mean not a little bit, but mostly. Is that okay?" Jasmine said shyly.

"Yes, perfectly ok. I need a boss...a Boss like you."

Jeet's words melted her heart into gold aqua regia. Folding her hands, closing her brimming eyes, tear droplets streaming down over her cheeks, slightly bowing down her head, Jasmine whispered with trembling lips, "O Mata Rani! Late, but you cared for me..."

Meanwhile, the counsellor and the two lawyers were perplexed witnessing the conversation between Jasmine and Jeet, riding over stormy and velvety emotions.

Her lawyer, though confused, gathered courage and asked, "Mam! Are you ok?"

"Don't you want me to be ok, Mr Lawyer?" Jasmine chirped like a sweet sparrow who had just survived ruining extinction and was blessed with a second chance at life.

"Yes, yes. I always want you to be happy. Keep smiling like this." Her lawyer smiled blandly.

"Then immediately do whatever I say. Inform the court to withdraw both cases which means cases against me and Jeetji. Start the process of bail and get us out of jail as soon as possible. And inform my parents to start the arrangements for our marriage. Fast...very fast." Jasmine blossomed in a positive mood.

Everyone got very delighted after hearing flowers and petals coming out of Jasmine's glowing face after long autumn.

Jeet added, "Yes, this meeting is over. Hurry up and do whatever Jasmine Madam has said."

*

So, a small positive thought, an innovative idea and a small calculated risk saved two lives from sinking into black holes and got a chance to flourish with flying colours.

In the very next hearing, the Judge was very happy to know that his idea, his suggestion brought miraculous changes to the twin case. He winded up the whole procession and passed on the final judgement—the acquittal of Jasmine and Jeet from the respective charges and the closure of the said cases. He didn't forget to congratulate Jasmine and Jeet on their amicably agreed marriage.

The news of this case was covered in local as well as national print media, digital media, and news channels and became a popular talk among the lovely Juhu Beach Lovers.

*

After one year, on one of the best days of their lives, Jeet and Jasmine's friends and families filled up their home with loud jubilations and celebrations on the arrival of new twin guests, wrapped like little bundles of joy.

Jasmine and Jeet unanimously decided to keep their names "Pyari" and "Dev" as a homage to the innocent departed souls.

*

Time was moving fast as ever. Another year passed by quickly without any control over anything around. Amid the babies' cooing giggles, twittering toots and trills, and cheeky chuckles, Jasmine and Jeet didn't forget the unforgettable date which changed their lives.

So, on the second anniversary of the unforgettable date, during the high noon hours, amid drizzling, the fairytale family of Jasmine, Jeet, Pyari, and Dev roamed around the significant locations, one by one. First, at the beach side 'S' curve turning near TAP Hotel and then at the other 'S' curve turning near Bora Bora Hotel and paid homage to Pyari and Dev.

The toddler Pyari sprinkled rose petals for departed Pyari at the spot near TAP Hotel.

The toddler Dev sprinkled jasmine petals for the departed Dev at the spot near Bora Bora Hotel.

Guiltless smiles sparkled over the faces of Jasmine and Jeet while looking into each other's eyes, drizzling droplets hid their tears this time. Seeing them smiling, Pyari and Dev too giggled with innocence.

And the family stayed happily ever after...

What a strange story.

In a single day, at the same place, happened two accidents, two untimely deaths. Two losers lost their lives and two losers lost their soulmates.

But, a prudent decision restored the spoiled lives again.

Was that a gimmick of destiny or the art of converting an adversary into serendipity?

Kudos to JUUHHHUUUU.

Don't forget to tell me how you found this story.

Keep enjoying walking around Juhu Beach. A lot of stories waving-in and waving-out every now and then.

Bye Bye

See you

JUUHHHUUUU

Hi Juhu Beach Lovers!

So, today, I am going to tell you a strange story, which happened at Juhu Beach, but it did not completely belong to Juhu Beach.

This story was told to me by Pyramid last year, during Navaratri—Durga Maha Navami.

In one line, this story is about "Not all smokes have their own fire".

***

Chapter 2

IMMERSIONS, EMERSIONS, EMOTIONS

Misty Juhu Beach

Outré October

Dawn

Drowsy sun, in somnolence, pandiculating in the sky, bidding adieu to the fading moon.

As always, all beach buddies were propped up on the dewy sand carpet but, that day, with a little bit of discomfort.

Boisterous tides were tossing myriad remains of immersed statues of Maa Durga at the beach, while the darkling tides emersed them in return.

The previous day was the last day of Navratri, and innumerable statues had been immersed the night before in the sea to bid a hearty farewell to Maa Durga. But, that morning the beach was full of emersed remains of statues and various other pooja materials. A team from the local Municipal Corporation was there to remove those remains from the beach in order to keep it clean and safe for visitors.

While routine beach activities were going on with caution, loud woofing noises attracted the attention of a few beach buddies. The noises were coming from the fierce fracas of a few stray dogs near a huge heap of remains. When they moved closer to stop the fight, they noticed that those stray dogs were fighting for a long piece of some sort of eatable, maybe some of the previous day's *prasada*, entangled in red residues of a statue, most likely Mahisasur, the Devil. But, when they looked more closely, they realized that it looked like a human leg, from knee to toe. A few chunks of it were eaten by the dogs causing it to bleed.

Someone somehow managed to drive the dogs away.

"Ohh! A leg. It's somebody's leg. Ohh," screamed a morning walker.

"Oh my god! What a horror," another guy screamed.

"Yes, yes. It's a leg. See the bone is also visible," the third guy yelled.

"Don't... Don't lose time. Let's call the police urgently," a lady cried.

A young boy rushed towards Juhu Police Station, just 500 meters away from the spot and informed what he had witnessed to the police staff. The police team rushed to the spot, barricaded that area, and started the process of *panchnama*.

Such a horrendous incident in the morning, shocked every passer-by and disturbed their rhythm of morning routines, resulting in the gathering of a huge crowd around that spot.

Soon forensic experts and the dog squad reached there and started their process. As a precautionary measure, police decided to check all the heaps of remains on the beach and instructed the municipal team to keep their cleaning process under hold till further instructions. Police soon covered the whole area with stout barricading and kept on driving the beach walkers to move away from the crime site and not to form any crowd, but people kept gesturing, unruly out of curiosity, to watch that human leg.

After some time, the police and the crowd were shocked when one after another a few more human body parts were found in a similar condition, badly mingled with idols of Mahisasur, Maa Durga and her ride, the Lion. First, the forensic team found something resembling a human nose, then an ear, then a hand, and, surprisingly, an artificial hand... Everybody was in dilemma about what the hell was going on.

Neither police nor the regular Juhu beach visitors had ever witnessed such shocking findings of human body parts, precisely speaking, out of the remains of the idols of holy deities. Though cases of the surfacing of dead bodies out of suicide or murder have been witnessed at Juhu Beach, nothing ever connected with such holy festivities.

Within a few hours, the news went viral on all social media platforms and started airing on all leading news channels, sending shock waves and causing chaos all across the masses. And then from a security perspective, the police sealed the entire Juhu beach area till further orders.

The samples were sent to the forensic lab for further investigations and nothing was found from the residuals of other holy idols.

The dog squad was sent to various locations where the Maa Durga's idols are made. But, that was a huge task. In Mumbai and Thane, there were more than 200 licensed idol makers spread across more than 50 locations.

*

A couple of days later, after receiving the final forensic reports at Juhu Police Station, SHO Bharat Singh was jointly reviewing those reports with his team. His team had already reviewed and actioned the further necessary processes. The findings of those reports surprised them more than the findings of those human body parts on the beach.

"What the hell is going on? It's really shocking!" SHO Singh confronted his team. "It seemed that those body parts belonged to a single deceased, whose main body was not found there. But, these reports are indicating that each body part belongs to a different person. It's so messed up. What does it mean? Did the culprit kill five people? Or did he amputate five victims? And then he hid the body parts in the holy idols." He looked at SI Jasmu Patil and asked, "What do the DNA reports say?"

"Sir, these DNAs didn't match with any past or existing cases of unclaimed corpses or any murdered or amputated victims. They don't even match our records of accidentally injured or deceased. And not even anybody who died of normal death," she responded.

"SI Shinde, what are the findings from the dog squad investigations of the idol makers' locations?"

"Sir, we visited all the locations in Mumbai and Thane. But, we haven't found any leads."

"What about the investigation of tags? Generally, the idol makers fix a tag on the idols, displaying their name on it."

Sir, we checked that also. But, on that particular idol, and the main idol of Maa Durga, there were no tags," SI Shinde said.

"That means those idols were not made by any authorized idol maker, but by some unregistered idol maker. Do one thing, find out how many unregistered idol makers are in this business. Not only in Mumbai and Thane but in entire Maharashtra and the neighbouring areas of Gujarat also. Fast! Fast!"

"Yes, Sir."

"And then use the dog squad to confirm the culprit."

SI Shinde nodded and left with his team for the assigned task.

SHO Singh asked SI Jasmu Patil, "When the DNAs are not matching, what is the next step? What to do to find the culprit?

"We should take help from other states, even from neighbouring countries."

"Other states, I can understand. But, why from neighbouring countries?"

"Because, Sir, the DNA patterns in these reports don't match with Indian patterns!"

"Hmm. Surprising! Very surprising! It means this case might have a foreign angle?"

"Yes, Sir. Definitely."

"Ok, carry on. Do whatever you are required to do. Now, what about that artificial hand?"

"Sir, we enquired with all the Indian manufacturers. But, everybody denied supplying that particular piece."

"Why?"

"Sir, as per Indian standard guidelines, each artificial body part bears a particular unique ID, allotted by The Artificial Limbs Manufacturing Corporation of India. And in this case, that artificial hand doesn't bear any ID on it. So, it's suspected that it might be supplied by some foreign manufacturer."

"What are you saying? Foreign manufacturers also follow similar guidelines. Actually, those guidelines are provided by WHO for manufacturers across the world. You must know this. I think these manufacturers are misguiding you. Any crooked fellow might have sold illegally, without the ID. That's why they are dumping the blame on neighbouring country manufacturers and misguiding us. Call them and ask them to meet me, one by one."

"Yes, Sir."

"And one more thing, what's the update on checking with hospitals and other police stations for any cases of amputations or accidents where the victims might have lost a leg, hand, ear, or nose?"

"Sir, we checked with all hospitals, all police stations, and HO Mumbai Police and Thane Police, but no such cases have been reported recently. We even checked with quacks but found nothing.

"Oh, God! Then how will we find the victims and the culprit? Strange case."

Later on, SHO Singh, accompanied by SI Jasmu Patil, had meetings with all the manufacturers of artificial body parts and Artificial Limbs Manufacturing Corporation of India but without any concrete results that would satisfy the legal points of view of the case.

After completing the investigations of unauthorized idol makers, SI Shinde also submitted reports, but nothing useful was found.

*

Days passed by quickly. Rumourmongers made Juhu Beach an unsafe and the scariest beach.

Footfalls went down drastically, and regular beach walkers also shied away in big numbers.

Juhu Police neither found the victims nor the culprit. All round pressure was building up on Juhu police and Mumbai police as well. The image of the police was being tarnished in news and social media for their failure to catch the culprits and resolve the case. Finally, they declared a reward of ₹ 50 lakhs for the person who catches the culprit or gives the police any information about them.

Even then, a few weeks passed by without any positive outcome. The desperate police then raised the bar and hiked the reward money to one crore rupees.

*

One fine morning, SHO Singh got a call from Mumbai Police HQ, informing him about a mass murder incident at Bandra where five amputated dead bodies were found. Earlier, the society secretary informed the police after noticing a foul odour coming out of an apartment in that building. To their surprise, the apartment was not locked from the inside, but something was pushed against the door. On pushing the door a little harder, the police noticed a dead body blocking the gate. On further inspection, they found rotten corpses lying haphazardly in different rooms throughout the apartment and a lot of blood-stained weapons lying near each dead body. Some mobile phones, electronic gadgets, documents, religious materials, essentials, kitchenware, clothes, etc., were also found in the apartment.

SHO Singh was asked to check the correlation of this case with the Juhu beach case, who rushed along with SI Jasmu Patil and her team carrying all the records to the Bandra crime scene.

All hell broke down when SHO Singh's team found a 100% match of the body parts found in Juhu with the amputated bodies at the Bandra crime site.

After a few days, it was found that the interim DNA reports of those dead bodies matched with DNA reports of the respective amputated body parts.

Though Juhu police were a little bit relaxed after the victims had been found and identified. But, the background information about them gathered so far from secret intelligence sources was immensely shocking and terrifying, which disturbed the course of the investigation and led to different perspectives.

Those five dead people were not from Mumbai, not even from India. They were from Pakistan. They entered India via Dubai as illegal immigrants. The leader of the gang, Bakhsh Pasha, used to visit India unabatedly for some time now.

His father, Rassool Pasha, was a self-proclaimed social worker; mediocre businessman-cum-low profile underworld don of Karachi, Pakistan; and suspect of many cross-border terrorist activities in India. Rasool's social works were limited to serving a few radical religious groups only. He was enjoying the local public support too.

Rassool often kept Bakhsh with him for training him in all the tricks of his businesses. Finding Bakhsh dead in a foreign land surprised authorities back home in Pakistan. In the underworld, Bakhsh was infamous to be a rogue, spoilt brat. A fierce fight with rival gangs cost him losing his right hand, and then Rassool illegally arranged an artificial hand for his son from the black market of Pakistan itself.

But, the Indian Police couldn't find the purpose of Bakhsh's frequent illegal visits to India. The Pakistan counterparts, as ever, were not cooperating fairly in this matter for the best possible reasons known to them. They denied identifying the dead as belonging to Pakistan. But, the Indian police didn't stop there and were trying their level best to crack the mystery by taking the help of Indian secret agents and a few international agents too.

Prima facie, the Indian Police, CBI, and RAW were struggling to unfold the mystery behind the murder of Bakhsh along with his five associates. They waited for the final forensic and investigation reports covering interrogations of many local anti-social elements too, for reaching a convincing conclusion about this mass murder mystery. The unknown reason behind the gruesome crime was also bothering them like hell.

Days were passing by one-after-another and the pressure was building up like anything. Media was consistently behind the police, scratching their heads for break-through. Social media was being flooded with trolls against the police for their failure in nabbing the culprits and closing the case.

After a few weeks, the final investigation reports shocked the whole police department, CBI, and RAW and blew off their wild guesses into sheer embarrassment. This report was concluded from various reports: post-mortem, DNA, forensics, secrets agents, and dog squad reports; mobile call records (mobile sets were from Pakistan but had Indian SIM cards and bore names of locals); data from mobiles; interrogations of society members, estate agents, mobile operators, and locals on whose names the SIM cards were issued, etc.

The final story which came out by joining all the dots was quite strange and unbelievable. Mumbai Police, in the presence of Juhu Police, narrated their version of the story at the press conference.

Bakhsh Pasha, son of a Karachi-based don, Rassool Pasha, was illegally visiting India for a few months with the support of Indian counterparts of radical religious groups. The purpose of his frequent visits was not his participation in activities like terrorism, religious hatred or anti-India activities, but something else, which he didn't disclose to anybody. That mystery was still a roadblock in the overall investigations.

The post-mortem and forensic reports indicated that the amputation took place a few days before Durga Maha Navami. The culprits and the location of the incident were still not known. The most shocking fact was that, even after getting severely injured and losing body parts, they didn't contact any doctor or hospital for their treatment. Rather they returned home and tried self-treatment. Herbal materials found in the house and traces of herbal coatings over their injured body parts clearly indicated this. They might have avoided contacting any doctor or hospital out of their fear of getting exposed. That's why the police didn't get any information about the incident before the body parts surfaced at Juhu Beach.

The amputated body parts, along with the artificial hand of Bakhsh, were hidden inside the statues of Mahisasur, Maa Durga, and her ride, the lion, and then smartly immersed into the sea at Juhu Beach. The residuals of the idols cluttered the beach the next day and led to people finding the body parts, which eventually started this case.

As investigations were not getting any significant breakthroughs, the police declared a reward for providing them with any sort of leads. Days passed, but nobody came forward with any information.

One fine morning, the society secretary called the Bandra police, revealing the locations of the dead bodies of the victims. Combining all the reports, the mystery that unfolded is much more shocking.

After the announcement of hiking the reward money to one crore rupees, Bakhsh started facing a revolt by a few of his gang members staying with him. The gang was divided into two groups—the greedy group who wanted to contact the police through their Indian counterparts, preferably politically strong mediators, to reveal the information about the culprits who injured them and get the reward money and, additionally, to get the government's pardoning for their illegal immigration to India. As per them surrendering and getting reward money would be better than worthless death or long-term jail. Whereas, the other group of Bakhsh's gang was adamantly against that suicidal idea.

The tussles escalated to the highest levels of betrayal and conflict leading to irreconcilable points of no return and ending in fierce physical fights. Then gruesome mutual lynching killed them all, where one badly wounded and bleeding guy, while trying to flee away, succeeded in opening the door bolt but collapsed before he could pull the door open. Thus, blocking anyone from pushing open the door from the outside even though it was unlocked.

When the reporters doubted the story, calling it unbelievable, and asked about the basis on which the police concluded that the internal fights led to deaths, the response from the police spokesperson was quite quirky.

First, the call records had traces clearly indicating the build-up of opinions regarding the reward money and telephonic complaints about each other.

Second, videos and pictures of gang members fighting and injuring each other were found on two mobiles, which indicates that two guys were recording the ongoing fight. Those pictures and videos would be vital proof in court for supporting the police investigations.

Somehow the Juhu Beach Amputation and Murder Mystery was partly resolved, even without any direct contribution from the police. The victims' fights exposed themselves. Now, police started looking for the hidden culprits, who amputated those dead victims.

*

Many days passed, but unfortunately, the police didn't make any progress with the case. Those bitter crooks were blemishing the image of the police very badly, such that Juhu Beach tourism was suffering because of that scary incident, unruly movements of foreign anti-social elements, and the delay in finding the culprits and closing the case.

In a high-profile meeting, it was decided to raise the bar of the reward money. Now, it was two crore rupees. Again, a few days passed, but there was no respite for the police.

But, one fine morning, on-duty police staff and a few visitors at Juhu Beach Police Station were surprised to see SI Jasmu Patil jumping out of her chair and talking loudly on a call.

"Saab, I want to talk about that two-crore prize money. I have the information..." a shivering anonymous voice spoke.

"Ok. Please tell me, what information?" SI Jasmu Patil immediately sensed that the call was a game-changer and face-saver for the police. Immediately, she signalled her team to record and trace the location of that call.

"Madam, if you don't mind, can I ask when will I get the prize money?" the anonymous voice asked in a fearful voice.

"Immediately," SI Jasmu Patil responded quickly.

"Immediately means?"

"Hmm... By cheque, once your information is found to be true. Maybe in a day or maybe in a couple of days after that. This is prize money declared by the police, so you must have trust. See, the police never let down those who help them in solving a case," SI Jasmu Patil cautiously reverted.

By that time, the team silently informed SI Jasmu Patil that the call location was very close to the police station.

"Ok, Madam. So, when should I meet you?"

"Any time. We can even meet now."

After the telephonic conversation, SI Jasmu Patil turned back immediately to rush to SHO Singh to inform him about this surprising good news but collided with Singh who was standing just behind her. Actually, Jasmu's loud reaction shocked him, so he came out of his cabin and was listening to her.

After SI Jasmu caught her breath and both of them apologized for the collision, she briefed Singh about the call.

A few minutes later, a middle-aged man, bearing the looks of a Hindu priest, along with a young couple, entered the Juhu police station. The man told the help desk that Madam had called them in for a meeting.

The issue being very sensitive, they were brought into the special investigation room. SHO Singh, accompanied by SI Jasmu Patil and a couple of senior associates, started the process of investigation with the trio of nervous informers, sitting in front of them with fearful faces.

SHO Singh started the conversation. "So, who called up?"

The salt-and-pepper-haired priest, bearing a wild bushy beard, in a weak husky voice, said, "Sir, I called up."

SHO Singh stared at the priest with penetrating eyes. Then, after a pause, he looked at the young couple. "Who are they?"

Priest, now with a mild smile on his wrinkled face, said, "Sir, we will tell you everything. First, let me start by telling you about myself."

"Ok, go ahead."

"Sir, my name is Pandit Ram Shashtri. For the last 35 years, I have been staying in the Hanuman temple at the farthest end of Juhu Shivaji Nagar slums.

Actually, the temple is far away from the slum colony, in an isolated location, surrounded by thin jungle and a few feet high rocks. There, long ago, a rock that looked like Lord Hanuman was found under an old banyan tree by some people. At that time, I had just started living in that slum with a few neighbours. After they came to know that I am a Pandit, they asked me to offer worship there. Finding it to be a lonely and peaceful place without any disturbances, I decided to settle down there. I developed this temple slowly over the years. It is not a very famous temple and witnesses a very few local slum devotees, who randomly visit here, and hardly any new visitors.

From the outside, the structure of the temple looks like a normal building with unplastered walls and without any lockable door. But, it doesn't have any roof, because of a lack of funds. It doesn't have flooring either. In monsoon, I put tarpaulin as a roof, to protect myself.

My livelihood depends mostly on the offerings from the devotees, though I cultivate a few vegetables and grains on that piece of land.

For 35 years, I have been staying at the temple only. I don't go anywhere. But, whenever I get an offer for sponsored pilgrimage, I graciously accept. And on those days, the temple remains open, though without routine worship."

SHO Singh was listening patiently to the priest but was getting irritated as he could not find any connection with the case. He intervened, "That's fine. But, what is your connection with this case? What is the information that you have about this case? And, by the way, which place do you originally belong to?

"Sir, I am from Nepal. But, right now, I am settled here only. I have everything—Aadhaar Card, Voter ID, Ration Card, etc."

Surprised SHO Singh grunted, "Hmm. Nepal. Ok, then what?"

"Yes Sir, that was about me. Later on, I will speak again. But for now, please let these young people tell you about themselves."

SHO Singh stared at the young couple and curiously gestured for them to start.

The young man hesitantly started in an ultra-soft voice, trembling with fear. "Good morning, Sir. My name is Romeo Montague. I was studying Arts, Final Year..."

"'Was studying', means? And tell in detail: which college, which city?" SI Jasmu finally spoke.

"Let him finish. Then we will start asking questions," SHO Singh told SI Jasmu.

Romeo resumed hesitantly. “Yes, Sir. So, till recently, I was studying BA Arts, final year. But, unfortunately, I was forced to quit due to some dire situations in life. Sir, actually, I am an orphan from Myanmar...”

The moment he said Myanmar, SHO Singh, SI Jasmu and the associates started getting bad vibes about how the situation was unfolding. First Pakistan, then Nepal, and now Myanmar.

Romeo continued, “Sir, I have been brought up in an orphanage run by Yangon Catholic Church in Yangon, Myanmar. I studied in a school and college on the campus of that orphanage, run by the same church. Since childhood, I had an immense interest in Arts, particularly drawing sketches, paintings, making sculptures, and sand arts. And with the blessings of God, I earned a very good name at the national level in school and college.

Meanwhile, at the SSC school level, I was selected for the Orphan’s International Arts Competition organized by ACD held in Myanmar itself.”

“By the way, what is this ACD?” SI Jasmu intervened.

SHO Singh stared at her and, through eye contact, asked her not to disclose her own poor knowledge.

Romeo continued humbly, “Madam, ACD means Asia Cooperation Dialogue.”

Despite SHO Singh’s continual rebukes, Jasmu grunted uncontrollably, “Hmm.”

By that time, Romeo understood Jasmu’s unworded query and responded, “Madam, ACD is just like you know SAARC, the South Asian Association for Regional Cooperation and ASEAN, the Association of Southeast Asian Nations. SAARC covers South Asian countries and ASEAN covers Southeast Asian countries. ACD covers all Asian countries.

Then he took a pause and inquisitively stared at SI Jasmu. SHO Singh asked him to continue. In fact, he was quite impressed with the narration style and knowledge of Romeo, and so were the others.

“Yes, Sir. So, my paintings were appreciated by many people. On the final day of the Award Function, I was very happy for the first time in my life, when I was declared the first runner-up. Though I was also unhappy at that time for not winning the first position, when the winner was declared, I just got mesmerized by seeing her.

The winner was Laila, a graceful girl with a bright smile. She was rushing to stand on the stage. I don't know why, but soon I was feeling even happier, standing beside her. I forgot my pain of losing the first position and was feeling excited for her."

Vibrant SI Jasmu couldn't control herself. She smiled sarcastically and asked, "Who is Laila?"

SHO Singh again gestured asking her to restrain herself.

But this time Romeo blushed and, gesturing towards the girl sitting beside him, whispered, "She is Laila."

This time, SHO Singh also couldn't stop himself. He stared at that girl and grunted. "Oh!"

SI Jasmu smiled but didn't say anything.

"So, Sir, that was our first meeting. We greeted each other and then departed. There, in my room in the orphanage, I couldn't forget her. I kept thinking of her bright smile and beautiful graceful face. Somehow, that year passed.

The next year again, I was selected for ACD Art Competition. That year it was being held in Bangladesh. There I couldn't stop myself from introducing myself to Laila. We exchanged our contact numbers. That year, interestingly, I was the winner and Laila was the first runner-up. But, what I liked was that she was very happy for me.

So, our mutual liking and admiration for each other brought us a little bit closer. Even after departing to our home countries, we were in continuous touch. Then next year being Higher Secondary Board Exams, I was not sent to the competition. And the same was the case for Laila.

The next year, we were in the first year of BA Arts, again selected to participate in ACD Orphan's International Art Competitions. That time, it was in Mumbai, India. We worked very hard and won many awards. But, this time, we enjoyed ourselves a lot, particularly at Juhu Beach. We saw many beaches, but Juhu is Juhu. No other beach can beat it. We decided that whenever time permitted, we would visit Juhu Beach again and again.

The next year we were in the second year of Arts, again selected to participate in ACD Orphan's International Art Competitions. But that time it was in Pakistan."

The moment Romeo mentioned Pakistan, some unprecedented guesses sparkled in the minds of SHO Singh, SI Jasmu and the team. Something common appeared in their eyes, but they continued listening to Romeo.

Romeo continued, "But, Sir, please let Laila continue from here."

SHO Singh agreed.

Now, Laila, wearing a grim smile, whispered, "Sir, I am also an orphan, residing in Bangla Girl's Orphanage, Dhaka, Bangladesh. I was brought up there only. My schooling and college happened in the Girl's Madrasa run by the orphanage. Right now, I was also in my final year of Arts.

As Romeo told you, our experience of earlier competitions in Myanmar, Bangladesh and Mumbai was quite pleasant and memorable. But, in Pakistan, it was horrendously life-threatening. There, I was ogled by somebody who didn't seem cultured or educated. Initially, he appreciated me a lot for my paintings and sculptures and showed an interest in purchasing them. We told him that those artefacts were not for sale but for competition only. But, when he desperately followed us, I shared contact details of our orphanage from where he could purchase and that was the biggest mistake I made."

"His name was Bakhsh Pasha." This time SHO Singh interrupted.

"Yes, Sir."

"So, now the whole story is getting clearer in my mind. But, you continue," SHO Singh said.

Laila resumed, "After returning from Pakistan, my life became hell. Bakhsh often used to visit Bangladesh, and every time he would come to our orphanage. He used to purchase my paintings and sculptures.

One day, he expressed his actual desire. He was never interested in my artefacts. He was just interested in me. He wanted to marry me. But, I had seen his mannerisms and psychic behaviour. I hated him. So, I bluntly refused. That's when he started showing his true colours.

He was a rogue, spoilt brat, who belonged to an infamous family of underworld dons, radical religious activists in Pakistan. So, after my refusal, he used all kinds of pressure tactics in Dhaka, using his radical religious and anti-social local contacts. Every now and then, he would pressurize me, the warden, and even the head of the orphanage. A couple of times, he had been arrested also. But, he didn't give up and continued with his devilish tactics to get me. Life became hell.

Somehow, that year passed. This year, in my final year of Arts, I was living a fearful life, being cautiously protected by the orphanage authorities. The Art Competition was in Nepal. Amid fearfulness, I somehow completed the competitions and was returning to Bangladesh by road on a hired bus. Romeo was also travelling by bus only, to Myanmar. At the border, our buses were halted for immigration checks.

Suddenly, I got a call from my roommate from the orphanage. I was shocked to know that a few minutes ago, Bakhsh Pasha had come there along with some local goons and quarrelled with Head Maulana. During the arguments, he shot Maulana to death and ran away threatening them with more dire consequences, if I didn't marry him.

Further, she told me to not come back here for a few days. Once things settled down, then only they would plan my return or I might also lose my life. She told me to find a safe shelter for the next few days.

I was shocked and I wanted to cry, but I couldn't get any voice out of my choked throat. Suddenly, I started feeling like spewing. I got off my bus and ran towards the roadside washroom. My colleagues were watching me in that uncomfortable situation. When I came out of the washroom, I saw Romeo standing outside, waiting for me.

Dealing with the sudden emotional outburst in a life-threatening situation, I held his hand and ran behind the washroom. I asked him, 'Will you marry me?'

He didn't utter a single word. He just pulled me gently and hugged me very tightly, rubbing my back, he whispered, 'Here in India, or in Bangladesh, or in Myanmar?'

My cries soared, but this time not in pain but in soulful happiness, at his uninquisitive, unconditional, innocent submissiveness to the words of a girl in pain.

I told him everything in detail.

Actually, we knew each other for the last five to six years and had been in continuous touch. We talked often, chatted a lot, and had mutual respect and admiration for each other. But, never had I looked at him as a potential love interest. To me, he was a very good artist, a good human being, a gentleman, and a well-behaved friend. I never saw him getting angry, though he got upset on a few rare occasions when poked insanely. But, he never reacted absurdly. We had also spent lonely moments during the breaks in the Art Competitions, but he never made any inappropriate gestures or tried to take any undue advantage. He never tried to touch me or seduce me. Though he did touch me, rarely, those were good touches. In fact, I used to see him as a brotherly figure. But, the dire situation changed everything within a second.

So, we quickly decided to first take out our luggage from our buses and take another bus.

While taking out my luggage, when asked by a colleague, I responded that it was an emergency, and I would be coming by another bus. I ran towards Romeo's bus standing in front of mine, where he was taking out his luggage.

We then decided to cool down first and discuss what next.

We sat in a nearby tea stall and while sipping hot tea, we started discussions. I asked him where we should go.

Romeo thought for a while and started eliminating our options. 'See, we can't go to Bangladesh. We can't go back to Nepal as the Visa has expired. We can't go to Myanmar for marriage as the church people will be against inter-religion marriage. So, we should go to India. India is far better than any other country, in terms of tolerance and accommodativeness.'

He was right. So, I asked, 'But, where in India? We don't know anybody there, and India is a costly country. We don't have much money.'

He said, 'When God has destined us to meet, he will arrange everything else too. Don't worry.'

'Have you fled from your homes?' Suddenly a piercing voice from behind us pulled our attention.

When we turned back, we found a middle-aged man, who looked like a Hindu priest, sitting behind us. He had been listening to our chatting.

He repeated the question. 'Have you fled from your homes?'

We both responded, 'No.'

'Then why are you talking like this?'

So, that person was Baba Pandit Shashtri. Now, Sir, kindly allow Baba to continue the story from here."

SHO Singh said, "Yes. Go ahead."

Pandit Shashtri: Sir, I was returning after visiting Lord Pashupatinath in Kathmandu, Nepal. While border immigration checks, on the Indian side, I was sitting at a roadside tea stall. Suddenly, a boy and girl came there, and without noticing me, they started their discussions, full of pain.

When they felt safe with me, they told me their story at length. I believed, the way they told me, their expressions and body language were genuine. I advised them to come with me and stay here till their issues settle down. They could find a good job too.

When we reached here, without any prejudices, for their protection and mine, I told them that if they married with Muslim or Christian rituals, it might sprout problems during their stay in the temple because the devotees might object. Even their enemies could trace them. So, I suggested they got married as per Hindu rituals, which will protect them from any unforeseen problems because more than abiding by religion or the system of marriage, protecting life was most important at that time.

Even after marriage, they had to ensure not to practice their religion. Because, again, that might have created suspicions in people's eyes. My intention was to protect their life and to give them support till they found their own arrangements. After that, they would have been free to start practising their own religious practices.

They understood and, without any reservations, agreed to my suggestions. So, I officiated their marriage in that temple through Hindu rituals. I also gave them Hindu names. Romeo became Raman, and Laila became Lalita.

They were living happily inside the temple campus, and I was staying outside the wall. Intermittently, they would go outside searching for livelihoods.

A few months passed by, and one day, I got a proposal from a devotee to go to Kolkata with him to see the famous Durga Navami there. I agreed and left for Kolkata, before the start of Durga Navami this year.

Now, let them continue from here."

SHO Singh gestured to continue.

Lalita aka Laila resumed. "Sir, after Baba's departure to Kolkata, we continued with the daily chores of the temple and spent time exploring job opportunities related to our skills. One night, while we were about to start having our dinner, cooked over the earthen *chulha*, a known voice pierced my ears.

'Smart girl! But how long will you run away from me?'

I froze. The moment I turned back with a lantern in my hand, my throat choked and there were goosebumps all over my body. It was Bakhsh with a bunch of goons at our doorstep. How the hell could he know our whereabouts?

'I have my spies everywhere. It had to happen sooner or later.' He looked at Romeo and asked, 'Who is this?'

Collating my strengths and showing him that I was not afraid of him, I said, 'Raman, my husband.'

'Husband? That too a *Kafir*? You are mine only. Only I can marry you, nobody else,' he yelled in extreme anger.

I also groaned. 'That was in past. Now, I am married.'

Bewildered Bakhsh suddenly went mad and screamed at his punters. 'Kill him! Kill him!'

Those four goons rushed towards us and started beating Raman very badly. Though he was trying to resist and protect himself from their physical attacks, he was not succeeding. Seeing that, I also jumped in and started beating them to rescue Raman from their clutches. But, I was finding it very difficult, to face a fight with four goons.

Then suddenly, Bakhsh slapped me with his artificial metallic hand, maybe to distract me from the action, but it hurt me severely and I was thrown away. I fell near a pile of firewood used for cooking food. While getting up, I saw a sickle lying there. In the dim misty light of the lantern, I got up holding the sickle behind me.

When Bakhsh saw me stand up, he rushed towards me and again raised his hand to slap me. But, this time, I surprised him and hit him with full force. To my shock, the sharp-edged sickle chopped off his metallic hand, which flew a few feet away and left him bleeding. He screamed in pain, holding the cut hand.

Seeing that, the four goons got distracted. One goon jumped at me and tried to kick me. I reacted by defending myself with the sickle. His leg was chopped off from the knee. He screamed in grave pain and fell down holding the bleeding leg.

Then the other three goons stood up as they watched their two severely injured friends. They left Romeo lying down on the floor, but by that time, I had gone fiercely brutal. I felt like I had become Maa Durga, on a spree of cleansing evils from this world. Without losing time, I hit another goon, and this time the sickle cut off his ear. He also cried out loud and fell down.

Another goon anguishedly rushed towards me, but I didn't give him a chance. I hit him hard on his face with my sickle, which cut his nose. He also yelled in pain and fell down holding his bleeding face in his hands.

Now, the last goon standing near Romeo, seeing all his gang members get injured, lost his control, jumped onto me, and tried to punch me in the face. I tricked him by swinging my head to the other side, and before he could have pulled his hand back, with full power, I hit him on that hand.

The sharp edge of the sickle cut his hand, which fell off, leaving him bleeding and crying out badly.

I couldn't understand what happened to me at that point in time, it seemed that Maa Durga had entered my body to punish those goons. Poor Romeo was shockingly watching all those actions with his broadened eyes full of sheer perplexity. But, I was not in the mood to spare them in any condition, waving the sickle in my hands, growling fiercely, I inched towards them.

Seeing that, severely hurt Bakhsh and his goons somehow stood up, screaming and yelling, and started leaving our home limpingly. But, my anger was so high, I challenged them by waving the sickle high in my hand. I drove them away with dire warnings. Barking stray dogs made them rush away in the dark night.

After that dreaded experience, we couldn't get any sleep. A lot of horrendous questions kept on storming us.

Firstly, whether to continue staying there or not? Because Bakhsh might come back again. But, we couldn't breach the trust of Baba, who helped us in our dire need. Then we decided to spend the nights at the farthest corner of the slum, where nobody visits at night hours.

Secondly, should we inform Baba over the phone? But, then we decided not to bother him while his Durga Navami festivities in Kolkata and tell him everything once he returned.

Thirdly, what to do with the chopped body parts? Earlier, we thought of throwing them in the adjoining sea as food for fish, but there were no fish, so we dropped the idea. Those pieces couldn't be thrown off anywhere as that could create suspicion and then it would become very difficult for us to defend ourselves. Those pieces couldn't be buried in a pit. Because stray dogs dig out any meaty material from any depth. Such kinds of incidents had happened over there a few times back as dogs dug up dead rats and other small animals. So we had been trying to find the safest way to get rid of those amputated human body parts.

Suddenly, the same idea came to both of us, almost at the same time. Why not make Maa Durga's statue and hide those pieces inside it? We will worship Goddess for the entire period of Durga Maha Navami, and then will do the immersion into the sea. If anything goes wrong, then also nobody could get to us in such a huge crowd of immersions.

So, the next day, we went to the market and purchased soil to sculpt Maa Durga's statue.

We had never made a statue that big. Gathering all our experience and knowledge from Art Sculpting classes, we made a statue and hid those well-wrapped body parts in different parts of the statue—Maa Durga, Mahisasur, and her ride, the Lion. As I am a Muslim and he is a Christian, we didn't know the worshipping process but somehow managed to do the prayers and perform the rituals following what we had learned from watching Baba. On Navami, we ourselves drove the hired hand cart and did the immersion in Juhu Beach along with many others devotees.

After some days, when Baba returned from Kolkata, we told him everything in detail. He immediately advised us to surrender ourselves to the police. But, at that time, we were very much frightened. So, we requested him to wait and watch. But, when the news of Bakhsh and the gang members' murder broke out, we felt very much relaxed. But still, fear was there. Because of Bakhsh's notorious criminal background, anybody from their side could harm us at any point in time.

But, later, when the prize money was doubled, we sensed the criticality of the situation. So, this time, we agreed to surrender. Now Baba can explain."

SHO Singh let out his breath, he didn't know he was holding. He looked at SI Jasmu Patil and his team and found them equally stunned. "Yes, please, Panditji."

"Yes, Sir. I told them to never ever think about running away from the law and the police. If someone has done a crime, they must surrender to the police.

Their one fear was that they are foreign nationals and had entered India and are residing here illegally. And chopping body parts is a highly serious crime. So, they were scared that the police would take strict action against them and they would get a severe punishment, maybe jail for a long time or they might be deported back to their own country, which could be unsafe for Laila. I convinced them that I was equally responsible for their illegal entry and illegal stay in India. So, I would also get the same punishment. And as far as chopping off body parts is concerned, that was not planned but was for self-defence only. So, I asked them to let the law take its own course and do justice in the right way. Finally, they agreed with the hope that the law would consider those facts.

So, have I done the right thing, Sir?"

SHO Singh replied, "Hmm. Yes, Shashtriji, you have done the right thing. But, it was a long long story. Not one story, but many stories.

Those body parts surfacing at Juhu beach, and the story travelling from Juhu beach to Pakistan to Bangladesh to Myanmar to Nepal. Wow! What a case! What do you say, Jasmu?"

SI Jasmu Patil smiled. "Yes, Sir, a very strange story. In this story there was everything. A love story expanding to two countries, a rogue one-sided lover-cum-villain from another country and a gentle helping hand from another country. So many twists and turns, love, madness, chase, attack, heroine's powerful retaliation, villain's suicidal adventure, Asian country's cultural programmes. But, in the end, who suffered?"

SHO Singh chuckled. "Juhu Beach and the police. Hahaha. People from foreign countries come to India without any knowledge about the country and do adventures here, while India is suffering. What a joke?"

He took a breath and continued, "Ok, jokes apart. Now, please listen to me carefully. Right now, all three of you will be arrested and will be taken into police custody. You will be prosecuted for the charges you already know. But, you surrendered to the police without hiding anything, thus, helping the police close this case. Particularly, Pandit Shashtri, who guided you both very well and brought you to the police. So, he will definitely be rewarded with the prize money. But only after clearing the court case against him for helping foreign nationals enter India and letting them stay here illegally.

So, guys, get ready to face the law. Don't worry, your case is not so complicated. I hope the court will definitely consider the conditions under which you committed the crime, your honesty, and your willingness to help the law.

Pandit Shashtri, Romeo, and Laila were arrested and prosecuted as per the provisions of the law.

*

Many months passed. One good thing, SHO Singh did was that he managed a low-profile closure of the case. He never disclosed the true identities of the accused and, thus, helped them by protecting them against their fears of further attacks.

For everyone else, the case is still going on as per the well-known fact that 'Law will take its own course.' But now, Juhu Beach has regained its faded glory and the footfall has increased to new highs.

What a cross-border story!

The scary amputated human body parts surfacing at Juhu Beach, hidden in holy idols.

Police investigations not yielding any results.

A mass murder exposes the victims. But, their credentials were much scarier from a National Security perspective.

However, the culprits were still at large. The police couldn't find them.

But, the lucrative reward resolved the mystery. Police got the culprits at their doorstep.

Critics and trollers fumed as the credit couldn't go to the police.

But, it was their idea to offer a lucrative reward, which drove all the characters to unfold the story themselves.

A strange web - Hero from Myanmar, Heroine from Bangladesh, Villian from Pakistan, Well-wisher from Nepal - all became a headache for the police in India.

But, in the end, who had the last laugh?

Kudos to JUUHHHUUUU.

Don't forget to tell me how you found this story.

Keep enjoying walking around Juhu Beach. A lot of stories waving-in and waving-out every now and then.

Bye Bye

See you

JUUHHHUUUU

Hi JUHU Beach Lovers!

So, today I am going to tell you a ghost story, which happened at Juhu Beach.

This story was told to me by Pyramid on Valentine's Day last year.

In one line, this story is about "True valentines have to face so many bitter truths of life".

***

Chapter 3

VIRTUAL VALENTINA

Smoggy Juhu Beach

Flirty February

Blushing Sun was hesitant to bid adieu as it requested Moon not to depart but stay back together that day.

Briny tides waving kisses to their soulmates, the brownie sugary diamonds.

As usual, beach lovers were flashing in one after another on the dewed sand carpet of Juhu Beach, starting their routine course of hobbies and then continuing flawlessly like a soothing breeze, except for someone who was not appearing as comfortable as all others.

As her routine, for the last few years, Jasmeena was enjoying her morning brisk walk, accompanied by her puppy Joho. But the last few days had not been the same. She felt being eyed and shadowed by somebody.

Sometimes, the brat was coming across from the opposite direction and staring at her shamelessly. Sometimes, he was following her at a very close distance without changing his awkward posture. Sometimes, he was standing with swag at some spot in her route as a roadblock.

For the initial three days, she didn't notice out of her careless and cool attitude, or she didn't mind any stray stud drooling around. But, when the guy frequented abnormally, her sixth sense alerted her to some unforeseen absurdity building up around her. She started observing that guy attentively without hinting at him.

What she found was not a usual kind of eyeing and crisscrossing but seemed to be a well-orchestrated modus targeted on her by someone anonymous for unknown reasons. The tom-boyish careless middle-aged feminine fashion designer suddenly found herself in jitters, which she hates most. Her mind was struggling very fast to get rid of that ongoing filth around her.

On the fourth day, she lost her patience when she saw that eerie shadower, silently eyeing her from some distance. Annoyed, Jasmeena outrageously prompted her puppy to attack the guy. But, to her surprise, Joho woofed again and again cluelessly.

She yelled while signalling for the target. "Joho! Go get him. Attack him!"

But, the obedient Joho wouldn't react. He kept on staring innocently at her while yipping as if asking, 'Where?' The puppy's inability to notice the culprit and react made her anxious against her nature. In fact, it escalated her annoyance. She was not in the mood to spare that bastard who was making her life hell.

Reddened Jasmeena, instead of reacting directly in her tomboyish style, preferred taking help from the police. So, she slowly inched towards the Juhu Police Station, parallelly keeping watch on that guy, who was consistently following her from a safe distance. After reaching there, she briefed the police in a few words and convinced them to come and help her.

"Where is that brat?" asked the police constable after coming out on the beach.

"Constable Saab, look there, he is there only, looking at us. The bastard is smiling too," Jasmeena exclaimed loudly.

"Where, Madam? Where? I can't see anybody there," the police constable responded in helplessness.

"What you are talking about Saab? You can't see? It's surprising. Ok, let's go to the spot itself. There you can catch him."

They started moving towards the guy.

So, it was the first occasion that she was standing very close to him. She couldn't tolerate his sarcastic smile. She turned towards the police constable and asked. "Saab, now you see him? He is just six feet away, arrest him."

"But, Madam whom should I arrest? I need somebody to be there to arrest. When there is nobody, how can I arrest? I feel there is some problem with you. You better consult a doctor. Ok, I am going back. I will report to SI. You can meet him afterwards." The constable's reply perplexed Jasmeena with sheer annoyance, who stared at him in utter disgust.

First, loyal Joho wouldn't obey her instructions. Now, the stout sharp police constable can't see that guy. Something weird was happening, her mind signalled. Frustrated, Jasmeena whispered to the constable who was turning to leave. "Ok Saab, I will meet the SI."

She stayed there, watching the constable go away while she kept shifting her eyes on and off of that mysterious guy.

A few minutes later, when the constable had gone, with fiery eyes, she turned back to that shadower and angrily shouted at him. "Who the fuck you are? Why are you after me? What do you want? Speak up. Open your mouth, I say."

People moving around were surprised to see her behaving insanely like that.

The hooded shadower was just smiling while keeping eye contact with Jasmeena, without blinking.

His weird response maddened her further. She shouted at her loudest, "You bastard! Answer me. Answer me, or else I will kill you right now."

The shadower kept on smiling, irritating her further. She lost her control and rushed towards him. Joho was watching her amusingly and followed her. She crossed those six feet in a fraction of a second. Just a couple of inches away, collecting her strength, she blew a punch over his face.

The sound of the quick move refracted in the air and she stumbled beyond that guy, almost passing through him. She managed to keep herself from falling down, but that guy remained standing still wearing a mysterious smile. Watching that, her eyes broadened in surprise with the scariest curiosity.

"Are you ok? Do you need any help?" A sweet voice of a passer-by lady distracted her ongoing thoughts.

She saw a few more people watching her, surprised.

"No, no, no. I am ok. Thank you," she responded humbly.

She calmed herself. Rubbing her hands, she started self-talking. *But what exactly happened? I blew a heavy punch on his face, but then the force drove my whole body through his body. How can it happen? How could I pass through his body? Oh my god! Is that guy a ghost? Why is he shadowing me frantically for the last few days? Whatever. First, I should leave this place immediately. Then, I will decide what to do with this ghost.*

"Joho, come on! Let's go."

Then, without giving another eye to that ghostly guy, she moved away from the spot and headed towards her car parked near the great Chhatrapati Shivaji Maharaj Memorial Statue.

Somehow she managed to drive while feeling like a million needles penetrating her head, which was aching beyond toleration. Her eyes were burning like fireballs, lips shuddering with the unquenched fire of abuses, hands shivering in sheer annoyance. All woes rose suddenly when at the first signal, she saw the same shadower surface in front of her car, gesturing for a lift with a sarcastic smile on his face.

"Oh my god!" yelled out scared Jasmeena. She pressed the accelerator of her automatic car, broke the signal and drove away, ignoring the complaining travellers behind. She wanted to reach her apartment as early as possible, which was only two kilometres away from Juhu Beach.

*

Jasmeena was so upset that even after reaching home, she couldn't snap out of the embarrassment she faced earlier that day. She went for a shower to cool down. Joho was a little bit disturbed as well, seeing the mood of his beloved mom.

After having a shower, with a coffee mug, she came into the sea-facing balcony of her apartment on the 11th floor. Looking straight into the horizon, she swallowed the first sip of her favourite filter coffee.

As she was going to take another sip, she turned her head to her right, and the coffee gushed out of her mouth, her eyes popped open, and her hands shivered as the coffee mug slipped and fell.

"What the hell is going on?" she whispered when she saw the shadower standing below a light mast just 100 feet away from the building.

Frozen, Jasmeena lost her patience, when she saw that guy come toward the building, walking on the sand bed. He then stopped to lift the mug and looked back at her and smiled. Now, she got scared seeing his eerie didoes. She turned back swiftly, closed the balcony door, and dumped herself into the sofa in the living room.

Whatever weird things she had faced since morning was hurting her so badly that they brought tears to her eyes. Though she had gone through severe hardships and heartbreaks in her life, never had she come across such kind of ghostly thing in her life. A lot of dark thoughts started storming her mind. *What the hell is going on? Who the bloody is this ghost? Though I don't believe in ghosts, the weird reality is that he is visible to me only. Why is he not visible to others? What connection does this ghost have with me? I have never had any ghostly experiences, not even anyone in my family. Then from where has this ghost come into my life? What does this ghost want from me? Does he want to kill me, but why? But, if he wanted to kill me, he could have killed me easily by now. He wouldn't have shadowed me like that? But, now what should I do? How to get rid of this unruly sarcastic anonymous jinx?*

After a lot of brainstorming, she remembered Meira, the Life Coach, whom she met a couple of times at page three parties and exchanged business cards. Quite popular in the upper middle class and high-class circles, as an Art of Life Trainer, Hypnotherapist, Reiki Healer, Crystal Healer, Energy Healer, Spiritual Healer, and a few more. But, in muffled voices, she was also known for secret esoteric practices, with a modern version of Witchcraft, Ghost Hunting and Tantrik kind of practices.

Without losing time, she called up Meira, briefed her about the problem, and asked for urgent help. Meira listened attentively, cancelled her all appointments, and assured Jasmeena of reaching her house in three to four hours with all needful arrangements.

As the morning ghostly infuriation already broke her and her meeting with Meira could be taking a reasonably long time to resolve the issue, she decided to inform the office of her absence for a critical personal emergency.

Soon after, she started getting calls from her colleagues and close friends with formal "Take Care" and "Get Well Soon" messages.

She didn't mind when a few expectant male friends optimistically reminded her of her owed promise of becoming their valentine that day. Despite her pissed-off mood, with an affiliative smile and a sugary mezzo-soprano voice, she managed to convince them over video calls that despite her willingness she couldn't make it because of an inexplicable personal emergency. She told them not to get disheartened and to keep on enjoying her memories.

Though those calls soothed her a little and diverted her mind from the grave situation she was in, she was feeling highly uncomfortable both mentally and physically. She was not even feeling hungry for breakfast and was not in the mood to watch TV. The only thing she could do was wait for Meira. There were still three to four hours to go. Puzzled Jasmeena asked Joho to become her pillow and then rolled over the floor and closed her eyes to avoid the scary world around her.

*

The ringing sounds of the doorbell and Joho's woofing awoke Jasmeena with a jerk. *Oh my God! How could I just sleep? Whatever. Let's see, maybe Meira has come.*

Yes, it was Meira, ringing the doorbell. Jasmeena welcomed her and soon told her everything in utmost detail. Meira listened to everything attentively. Then she wished to take a round of her house.

After completing the internal round, when they came outside, on the balcony, Jasmeena was shocked to see that guy still standing below that light mast holding her coffee mug.

She pointed toward him and groaned, "See, Meira, that's the guy, standing below the light mast. Since morning, he has made my life hell. See, how shamelessly he is staring at us."

Poor Meira, even though couldn't see anyone there, did wonderful acting as a shrewd esoteric practitioner and gestured with pseudo-professional egoism. "Don't worry, Jasmeena. I will not spare this ghost. It can't dare to bother you anymore. Today only this ghost will be out of your life. I have seen him properly. Now, come on, let's start the process of controlling the ghost. Come on in."

As soon as they came inside, Meira opened her bags and started arranging various items and materials to perform rituals to get rid of the ghost.

After completing the process, she tied sacred red-coloured threads over each door and window of the house, one thread on Jasmeena's wrist, and one thread as a necklace. Then she confidently assured Jasmeena, "These sacred red threads will enact as a safety barrier. Now, the ghost can't touch you, can't harm you, and can't even enter your house."

"But, what about the ghost appearing in front of me every now and then?"

"See, for today, please don't go to your balcony. Don't open the main door, even if the monitor shows any known person. Instruct the building security, not to disturb you even if someone has come to meet you."

"But, what about tomorrow morning? My routine morning walk at Juhu beach."

"Hmm. It's better if you go with your husband or your children."

"Actually, I am single. I am not married or have children."

"Oh! So you are single. But, why didn't you marry yet?" Meira said, surprised.

"I am very busy in my profession, so didn't get time."

Meira dug further. "How? What are you saying that you didn't get the time? At parties, I have seen you have many male friends."

Jasmeena boasted, “My persona is like that. Males get attracted to me naturally. I don’t invite them.”

“Oh, so now it seems to me that even the ghost got attracted towards you. Isn’t it so? Haha!”

As it seemed, Jasmeena didn’t take the comment well.

Meira immediately diverted the conversation. “Jokes apart, what I want to tell you is that it’s better if you don’t go for a morning walk tomorrow.

“But, that will give an impression that I got scared. My absence will encourage his insane morale.”

Meira laughed. “Oh! You don’t want to seem scared and don’t want the ghost to be happy about that. Ok, then, tomorrow morning, I would like to accompany you. I want to see how the ghost bothers you. Then, if required, I will do some more rituals at the beach to drive it away. Ok? Don’t worry. Now, it’s too late. I need to return home. By the way, what time do you go for the morning walk?

“At six.”

“Ok, don’t worry. I will come before that. But, I’ll come here only, at your house. Then we will go together to the beach.

"Ok. Thanks very much for helping me in such a dire situation."

"Oh, Dear! Don't worry, I am always there to help you. Ok. Bye bye. See you tomorrow. Don't come out of the house."

After Meira's departure, she immediately closed the door. Now, she was feeling very hungry, as she had not eaten a single piece of grain since morning. And poor Joho was also hungry.

"Oh, dear Joho, you also spent the whole day being hungry like me. Poor boy." She lovingly cuddled Joho and then cooked their favourite pasta.

After having food, she got in her bed to take much-needed rest.

While lying comfortably, before sleeping, she checked her mobile. There were 100s of calls and 1000s of messages. Mostly from the expectant male friends! She smiled with slanting lips, ignoring the pseudo-lovers. She closed her eyes to get some sleep in the early evening, around 7:30 pm. Tired Joho also closed his eyes.

*

After a few hours, Jasmeena was woken up after witnessing a nightmare. She was shivering. In her dreams too, she found herself being followed by that ghost.

Jasmeena whispered, "Joho! Joho! Lights..."

Hearing those words, even in pitch-black darkness, accustomed Joho got up quickly, moved towards the switchboard and pressed the button to put on the lights.

Jasmeena let out a loud scream when she saw that ghost sitting on the wooden stool placed in the corner. Joho got shocked. He couldn't stop himself from barking. He jumped in bed and sat beside her. She also held Joho tightly to feel safe.

"Surprised?" the ghost spoke with sarcasm. It was the first time he uttered something.

"How did you enter my house? What do you want? Why are you after me? Who the hell are you?" Jasmeena bombarded the ghost with questions in desperation, shrinking herself while sitting in bed.

The ghost stood up and started inching towards her.

Seeing that, she got frightened further and cried out. "How did you enter my house? Are you a ghost?"

Joho kept on barking.

The ghost came closer and sat in bed close to her

"Am I a Ghost?" He smiled with sarcasm. "Well, whatever I am, I am not harmful. You have many questions. I will answer all of them, but first, you have to answer my questions."

"No, no. First, you tell me. Who are you? Why are you after me? What wrong have I done to you? What enmity do you have with me?"

"First, you answer my questions, then you will get all your answers," repeated the ghost.

"But, how did you breach Meira's safety barriers?" Jasmeena couldn't control her inquisitiveness.

"Neither Meira nor Joho can catch me. Nobody can stop me from doing whatever I want to do. So, don't act like a kid. Now, tell me who is in trouble? You or Me?" asked the ghost.

"Me," whispered crying Jasmeena.

"So, you don't have any choice. Answer my questions, and then only you will get your answers. So, can we start?"

"Yes..."

"Good girl! But first, stop crying. You still don't look good while crying," the ghost said politely.

The word "still" raised curiosity in Jasmeena, but she didn't express it. Meanwhile, Joho was barking intermittently. Jasmeena signalled him to keep quiet.

The guy continued, "Tell me what date is it today?"

"14th February."

"What does this date stand for?"

"Valentine's Day."

"That's ok. But what importance does it have for you?"

Jasmeena thought a lot, but out of fearfulness, nothing was coming into her mind. Then she remembered the messages from her company, colleagues, and male friends. "Oh! Today is my birthday too! Oh my god, I forgot my own birthday because of everything happening."

The ghost chuckled, "What kind of a girl are you? You even forgot your birthday. Really very silly!"

"I am not a girl. I am a woman. Today I turned 47," complained Jasmeena.

"Ok, ok. Now tell me what else is there that has a connection with this date?"

Jasmeena thought a lot, but couldn't come up with anything. She finally gave up. "Sorry, I don't know."

"Ok, we will talk about this later. As you said, today you have turned 47, right? Now tell me, why didn't you marry yet?"

Hearing those words, her expression suddenly changed. It appeared as if her sore wounds were teased. Her beautiful face suddenly wilted down and darkened a little too. She held her face in her hands and drooped her head. She didn't utter anything. A few moments passed.

"I didn't hear anything," the guy said sarcastically.

Somehow, she handled herself and whispered, "It's a very long story."

"Don't worry, we have enough time. It's 9:30 pm only."

She started telling her story. "I was born and brought up in a beautiful city, Chandigarh. I was the only child of my parents. My father had a small shop for women's garments. My mother was a homemaker.

I spent my entire life in Chandigarh, in the same house in Sector 11. I did my schooling at Delhi Public School and then graduated in Arts from DAV College. I never ever visited any place outside of Chandigarh, because my father's business was never doing well, and he was handling it alone. But, I was allowed to enjoy life within the city.

So, I would often visit beautiful places like Rose Garden, Rock Garden, Sukhna Lake, markets, film theatres, and many more beautiful places.

My entire life in Chandigarh had one thing in common in each and every moment. And that was Dev... Dev Raj Singh. We were born on the same day. We lived in the same sector, but at the farthest corners. From nursery till 12th standard, we were in the same class. Then we joined the same college, though in different streams. He was my everything.

As my father had a shop for women's garments, I had a great fascination for dress designing. So, I joined Arts and Fashion Designing course. Dev's father had a shop for electronic goods like television sets, radios, mobiles, computers, laptops, etc. So, he had a fascination for electronics, especially computers. So, he joined Computer Applications.

We had one more thing in common, and that was simplicity. Since childhood, Dev was not a fashion-minded boy. He wore thick glasses and kept short hair, which was always oiled and combed. Though by the final year of college, he had turned half bald as the density of his hair thinned drastically. In his adolescent and young days, he used to wear a well-grown moustache and beard, rarely trimmed, and simple clothes. Though I had a fascination for fashion design, I also preferred to dress simply. Oiled hair, bare minimum simple accessories like nose pin, earrings, and a couple of bangles and simple girly clothes. In fact, we both liked the simplicity and sense of natural looks of each other.

During childhood, our friendship was known as a mere childhood friendship, nothing else. During adolescence age, we started celebrating Valentine's Day together. Never did we go for anybody else as our Valentine. The reason was our friendship and the common date of birth too.

During college days, we used to wander around the beautiful places of Chandigarh. Our parents knew about our friendship. But, they didn't have any objection. And, like me, he was also the only child of his parents. So, we were brought up in quite a pampered manner.

Our families were never engaged in family friendship because our parents were very busy and had hardly any time. So, often, only the two of us would visit each other's place.

During our final year, whenever we used to discuss our future plans, Dev would often say that he would go for a Master's to specialize in Software Programming. That meant it would still take him four to five years to settle down either at a job or build his own business. But, we were often blind about my career. I hadn't decided what I would do after my BA in Arts & Fashion Designing. Because there was the pressure of getting married and building up my home.

It was painful for both of us to even imagine anybody else as our life partner. During our journey together, we had become accustomed to each other. In childhood, we never saw each other from those angles. Even after adolescence, and till the final year of our college, we had a mutual feeling of friendship. But, we had never seriously thought of becoming life partners. Ours was such a soulful companionship, without any insane influence of immorality of sexual attraction or desires. In fact, since childhood, we were loyal, honest, and respectful towards each other.

I can show you our pictures."

She stood up, opened the cupboard, and took out an old album.

"See, this was our favourite picture clicked on our first Valentine's Day. We both were wearing blue jeans and a white shirt. Such a cute pair we were in those days.

One can get surprised that in a modern world, our love story was just a rubbish, non-existent fantasy. Because nowadays, children mature later and fall in love before that. More than that, young people don't even mind having multiple friendships and relationships with the opposite sex. They don't mind having sexual relations before marriage. But, our case was old-fashioned in the modern world.

That day, on Sunday, after sunset, we were sitting at the banks of Sukhna Lake. The thought of separation was worrying us. The news that the next day a prospective groom would be visiting me with his family was worse. We were thinking more and talking less that day. I was so sure about him. He was a shy guy and couldn't open up about his own needs. It was the need of the moment to decide something, or else our lives would be eclipsed behind irreconcilable agonies. Sometimes, he was blinking at me and then turning his head away. I was doing the same.

Suddenly, unexpected sensational words refracted in the air and echoed in our ears. 'Let's get married.'

Oh my god! Those words spurted out from our mouths at the same time, with the same emotion, with the same intensity. Now our eyes were glued to each other. After being together for almost 17-18 years, those were the very first moments when we felt the so-called boy-girl, man-woman, male-female love. The soulful expressions on our faces validated the sacredness of our love. For the first time in our life, we hugged each other very tightly. He kissed me on my forehead and so did I. We continued hugging each other for quite a long time,

A quirky voice disturbed us. "Don't do all this publicly. Go home and do whatever you want to do."

We realized the situation and immediately went to Dev's house. We clearly told his parents that we want to marry as early as possible. Though his parents were surprised, knowing our childhood friendship, they agreed without any resistance. Then we told them about the prospective groom's visit the next day and requested them to meet my parents immediately to propose our marriage. They agreed to that also.

After a couple of hours, we were at my home. Initially, my parents didn't welcome the idea. But, after some discussion, they agreed on certain conditions. The condition was to have a proper engagement, and the wedding should be held after final exams. Everybody agreed on that. A panditji was requested to come down to our place, even though it was almost nine pm. Again, he agreed.

After a lot of calculations and review of our *kundalis*, panditji informed us that the next day,

14th February, would be the most auspicious day for our engagement. Both families agreed on that.

So, the day, which started with a lot of tension, ended very well with loads of positivity in our life.

Two people born on Valentine's Day, who spent childhood and adolescence together as each other's valentines, got engaged on the auspicious Valentine's Day. I was very happy. Dev, too, was very happy. Both families were very happy.

After our final exams, the date of our wedding was finalized. All the preparations were in full swing on both sides.

The wedding was organized at a famous banquet hall. All the people, including me, were eagerly waiting for Dev's *Baraat*. Time was moving very fast. When some more time passed, and there was no sign of the *Baraat* coming, everybody started worrying. The blood pressure of my father was shooting up with the worst thoughts. Some people took their mobile numbers from my father and tried to contact them, but nobody was picking up. I also tried to call Dev, but he didn't pick up as well.

Suddenly, a relative hurriedly screamed, 'Let's go to Chandigarh City Hospital. Just now, I got Dev's father on call. He told me that Dev suddenly fell ill and has been admitted to the hospital. Let's hurry.'

My father, along with a few relatives, rushed towards the City Hospital. After a few hours, they told us that Dev was in a serious condition and was going to be operated upon very soon. The details were still not clearly known about what exactly had happened. His parents were continuously weeping in the ICU lobby.

Hearing that news, I couldn't control myself. I started crying. 'Why? Why? Why did it happen to us? Why and how can Dev fall ill suddenly? What the hell is going on?'

I kept on crying the whole night, intermittently taking updates of Dev. My mother and other relatives kept on consoling me. I don't know when I fell asleep.

My eyes opened when I heard my father's loud screams. 'They cheated on us. The boy was born with a physical deficiency. His treatment was going on since childhood. They didn't utter a single word about that. Even in the hospital, they didn't tell us anything. Thanks to the doctor who told us about the problem after a lot of requests.'

My mother asked curiously, 'What was the problem with Dev?'

My father yelled, "He had his heart on the right side, not on the left side like us. Doctors had already warned them after his birth. They couldn't say how long he would survive. Somehow, he survived till the age of 21. And now suddenly, on the wedding day, he got an attack. He is still in the ICU, still not operated on. Doctors are not sure about his survival. Doctors are waiting for the right moment for the operation. Till that time he is surviving on an artificial heart. Now, everything is finished. We can't let our daughter marry such a cheater, who hid such a critical thing from us.'

My mother was crying. All the relatives were abusing Dev and his family, cursing them.

I got very upset about that news. I was upset with Dev. Why did he never tell me this truth about him? Maybe his parents, out of protectiveness, hid this fact from us, from society. But Dev, who was very loyal to me, who honestly used to share everything with me, why did he hide that cruel fact?

Suddenly, I found myself surrounded by mixed emotions. On one hand, I was feeling sympathetic for my parents, who suffered such shameless deceit from Dev's family. There was a bitter, unpardonable feeling against the trust broken by Dev, whom I loved so much and with whom I spent the golden period of my life. But, on other hand, I was feeling sorry for him, who might be no more after some time. I found myself getting dragged into the biggest ever dilemma of my life and it couldn't be resolved until I talked to Dev, his parents, and the doctor.

The much-awaited happiness had vanished, leaving only sorrows behind.

Though my father had declared breaking the engagement, I couldn't forgive Dev so easily. After all, I couldn't allow anybody to spoil my emotional investment of 17-18 years. So, I couldn't stop there.

After a couple of days, I visited that hospital at odd hours and met the doctor privately. What the doctor told me again changed my perception of Dev.

As per the doctor, that deficiency in Dev was mentioned to his parents at the time of his birth. But, there was one more problem. Dev's mother got some severe gynaecological problems and couldn't become a mother again. On one hand, the child was born with severe life-threatening deficiency and, on the other hand, the hopes for another child had died forever.

To soothe the stress and increase the life expectancy of the child, the doctor advised the parents not to disclose that fact to the child.

Because, in such rarest of rare medical cases, the children suffered psychological depression and other life-threatening diseases once they came to know about their biological problems. He told them that whatever circumstances came in life, never tell the child about this, or else it could be fatal. But, one thing was sure, doctors couldn't predict how long such a patient could survive.

Even, the doctors doing the routine test at school were told to hide that fact from the student, his teachers, and anybody else.

After knowing all these new facts, my thought process, perception, and emotional angle towards Dev and his parents totally changed. Now, I did not have any complaints against them, but rather tons of sympathies. Now, I was eagerly waiting for his recovery, so I could meet him and talk to him.

When I shared these facts with my parents, they were not in the mood for any kind of reconciliation, rather were still against them. Their argument was that because of his medical deficiency, he couldn't survive for long and couldn't do anything in his life. So, I should stop thinking about him and marry someone else of their choice.

But, I didn't agree with their arguments and bluntly asked them if such a thing would have come up at a later stage, then what would their reaction have been. In that situation, one had to live with the facts of life only. So, I told them that I had decided to marry Dev only once he recovered and got discharged from the hospital. But, my parents kept on opposing my decision.

Though I was following up with the doctor, one day I got the information that Dev was taken to the USA for advanced treatments, which were not possible in India. His father had sold his properties in Chandigarh. His parents were badly humiliated by my father. That's why they were shy of meeting me while departing from Chandigarh, so they sneaked off silently. They didn't even leave any contact details.

That news broke me forever.

Later on, I refused all the marriage proposals brought to me. I clearly told my parents that only Dev could be my husband, nobody else.

Then, one day, I came to Mumbai to my close relative. She was into Fashion Designing. With her help, I started a new life, and today, here I am. I recently won the best Feminine Fashion Designer in Paris.

Meanwhile, my mother and father passed away in Chandigarh. So, I sold our properties there and settled here.

That's it about me. Now, you answer my questions."

"Ok, you told everything to me, crystal clear. A very emotional story. But still, I want to ask: Why you didn't marry? People around you think that you have many male friends, even close relations with many males," bluntly asked the ghost.

"See, as I told you earlier, a woman can't forget her first love. Dev was my first and last love. After he disappeared from my life, I never got those emotions for anyone else. And whatever people around me are talking about me are half-truths and half-lies. The half-lies are mostly passed by males out of envy and their frustrations for not succeeding in getting me for their vested interests. And the half-truths are like business formalities. I allow only those males to touch me or hug me whom I find absolutely innocent and have good vibes. People giving me bad vibes or oglers get kicks from me. I think I have clarified everything now."

"Hahaha... You are very particular about your demands. You are very mindful of your deliverables. Nice. Good, very good. So, now let me share my story. See, I am not a ghost, so no need to worry. You wasted your hard-earned money on Meira," the guy said politely this time.

"Oh! Means you are not a ghost. Then how come you entered my house without opening the door? And if you are not a ghost, then might be some alien," intervened Jasmeena.

"Oh! Keep patience, Madam! So, I am a Virtual Image. I think you might be knowing about Virtual Reality, Augmented Reality, Mixed Reality, and Extended Reality?" asked the Virtual Image.

"Ya! Definitely. We use it in our profession for presentations and meetings. But, I couldn't have guessed it that way. Because there one has to work within a frame and with the use of specific devices like VR headset, motion controllers, apparatuses, etc."

"Oh! You know these things, then also you couldn't catch the fact. The reason is that this is the latest advanced technology under the umbrella of so-called artificial realities. This technology provides you with a frameless, device-less, controller-less, user-dedicated environment and images to deal with. By using this, one can move the images and environments from any part of the world to any destination of own choice powered by satellite-controlled VPS. At the same time, one can restrict the visibility, voice, communications, interfacing and other actions of those images to selective users or selective targets by infusing digitalized footprints of DNA.

Right now, this advanced technology is not in public use, but rather a property of NASA. They developed this technology for their own space missions, new inventions, and maybe for some geopolitical uses also. So, that is all that I know about this.

Now, it is 11 PM. The time has come for you to meet the creator, who created me and used me for the last few days. This means, whatever was happening with you was well-planned and executed. The creator will explain everything to you."

"Creator? I don't get you. Who is the creator? And why should I meet him? And why was I chosen?"

"To get answers to your remaining questions..." said the virtual image and moved towards the main exit door.

Jasmeena followed. As soon as the door was opened, a guy with the same features as the virtual image was standing there, smiling with folded hands.

"So, Jasmeena Madam, he is the creator. Now, he will talk to you. Don't worry. In the end, you will be the happiest person today. Boss, now you take up," the virtual image politely said and disappeared.

The creator came inside with Jasmeena.

"Have you recognized me?" the creator asked in his husk voice.

"No! Maybe, because we never met," Jasmeena said.

"Oh! Really sad for me. But, I recognized you a few days back when I saw you at Paris Fashion Week. You won the Best Fashion Designer Award too."

"Oh! Nice. Are you also from Fashion Designing Industry?"

"No, no. I am not from Fashion Business. One of my friends requested I accompanied him to that event. Actually, I am from Cyber Technology Business. But, I am surprised that when I can recognize you, why can't you recognize me?"

"I am really sorry. I am trying to remember, but I can't. Can you give me some clue?"

"Ok, I will share one clue...Let's see what happens?" The creator took out an envelope from the pocket of his overcoat, took out a piece of paper and handed it over to Jasmeena.

Jasmeena's eyes broadened, cheeks blushed, lips shuddered, and she screamed in a sudden spurt of joy. "Oh! This is Dev and me. Our favourite Valentine's Day picture.

"Yes, Jasmi! It's me. Dev."

The creator's voice made Jasmeena jump and her eyes brimmed with tears with utter rejoicing. Words fluttered out of her shivering lips. "Jasmi! Only Dev used to call me Jasmi, no one else, not even my Mummy Papa. Dev! It's you. Oh my God! What a surprise! But, you have changed a lot."

"Time changes everything, Jasmi."

"Ya, it seems so. The last time when I saw you, you were lanky-shanky with a half-bald head, heavy moustache and beard, thick glasses, and simple clothing. And now, you are a little bit chubby, have great hair like film stars, no moustache, no beard, no eyeglasses, and even your clothes are very fashionable. Sorry, Dev. I think that's why I couldn't recognize you. And even your voice. At that time your voice was quite heavy, and now, what happened to your voice? It's unclear and husky. What happened to your heart problem? Oh, Dev! Oh, Dev!" Jasmi went on muttering in a flow of emotions. She hugged Dev very tightly and started crying with mixed emotions.

"Everything has been resolved now. No problem," whispered Dev and kept on patting her back to comfort her.

After some time, when Jasmeena calmed down, Dev held her face in his hands, looking into her moist eyes, whispered, "Do you remember, Jasmi, 26 years ago, on the same day, we got engaged and exchanged rings, but the cruel destiny separated us? We couldn't get married. Today is the same day, Valentine's Day. Even though we have grown old, let's get married.

"Let's get married," Jasmi screamed in her loudest voice and hugged him again tightly.

The lost lovers met again on Valentine's Day and moved out just before midnight to get married.

While on the way, Jasmi asked out of curiosity, "Why didn't you meet me directly? Why such a big drama of virtual reality?"

"Destiny's drama separated us, I thought let virtual drama unite us," whispered Dev while kissing Jasmeena.

Jasmeena's laughs sweetened the ambience as ever.

What a love story beyond ageing.

The day started with a morning walk shadowed by a ghost-like guy.

The ghost kept on haunting Jasmeena throughout the day.

But, the evening changed everything.

True lovers never depart. Destiny brings them back together.

What a love story, from childhood innocence to adolescence to engagement to a wedding that never took place to a broken engagement to a cruel departure.

But, Valentine's Day and their destiny brought them back together.

Now, they are ready to get married after 26 years.

Kudos to JUUHHHUUUU.

Don't forget to tell me how you found this story.

Keep enjoying walking around Juhu Beach. A lot of stories waving-in and waving-out every now and then.

Bye Bye

See you

www.ingramcontent.com/pod-product-compliance
Lightning Source LLC
LaVergne TN
LVHW091053150826
845673LV00002B/567

* 9 7 9 8 8 8 8 1 5 6 1 3 1 *